A NOVEL

CHRISTY DECKER

Enjoy!
With gratitude,
CD

Final 42

By Christy Decker

Cover Design by eLectio Publishing. Photo credit: Kara Miller.

ISBN-13: 978-1-63213-476-9

Published by eLectio Publishing, LLC

Little Elm, Texas

http://www.eLectioPublishing.com

5 4 3 2 1 eLP 22 21 20 19 18

Printed in the United States of America.

The eLectio Publishing creative team is comprised of: Kaitlyn Campbell, Emily Certain, Lori Draft, Court Dudek, Jim Eccles, Sheldon James, and Christine LePorte.

Publisher's Note

ACKNOLWEDGMENTS

I will always thank God first, for my life and for His goodness.

Secondly thank you to eLectio Publishing for another amazing opportunity in publishing this book. Jesse Greever and Christopher Dixon, it is an honor to work with your press again.

Part of the research process for this book included interviews with one police spouse and five police officers (all with the Austin Police Department.) They were very gracious in answering all of my questions and they gave me the inspiration for many of the scenes in this book. Thank you to Laura Delossantos (wife of Senior Officer Valentin Delossantos), Senior Officer Jennifer Durham, Senior Officer Ashley Edwards, Senior Officer Andy Mcrae, Senior Officer Will Moore and Senior Officer Ryan Nichols.

I want to thank all law enforcement officers who gave their all in the line of duty, especially Senior Officer Jaime Padron (Austin Police Department), Senior Officer Amir Abdul-Khaliq (Austin Police Department), and my husband's great-uncle, Officer Louis Kuba, who was killed in the line of duty after only two weeks of service in 1967 (Houston Police Department). I am eternally grateful for your service.

I also want to thank those of you who have retired from law enforcement, and thank those who are still serving, especially my dear friend and fellow Navy Veteran Officer Julie Daniel (Arvada Police Department), my cousin Senior Officer Jennifer Russell (Fort Worth Police Department), and my husband, Senior Officer Michael Decker (Austin Police Department.)

I've already mentioned my husband once in these acknowledgements but want to thank him again. Michael, your support is everything to me. I love you. Thank you for being my biggest encourager. To our half-dozen, F, C, S, T, B, & M, you already know that I love you all more than can be measured. Thank you all for inspiring me every day. Being your mother will always be my greatest privilege.

A final note for those who are reading, please remember the next time you have an encounter with a police officer to thank them for their service. They spend their work days protecting us, and they deserve our gratitude and respect.

FINAL 42

CHAPTER 1

SHE HAD ALWAYS BEEN INTRIGUED by the church she was entering now, as she had driven by it countless times before. She shuffled her way through the massive crowd of people, tilting her umbrella just enough to look up at a tall bronze sculpture of Jesus. He was standing at the edge of a boat, His arms stretched out as if to welcome everyone in. She had never been a religious person, but she had to admit, she felt an odd sense of comfort as her eyes were on that sculpture, passing it slowly, each step taking her to the place where the funeral would soon begin.

Sitting in the pew now, she sought that comfort again, but all she could feel was a heavy blanket of grief, so heavy it was difficult to sit up straight.

Her eyes wandered to the wood-paneled walls of the church as she sat uncomfortably, trying desperately to avoid looking to the front of the church, where the casket was. It was surreal, imagining his lifeless body in that big oak box. It wasn't how she wanted to think of him: a dead man forever gone from this Earth. She only wanted to imagine him alive. She wanted him to *be* alive. She closed her eyes and could see his smile. She slowly opened them again and couldn't avoid it—the American flag draped over his coffin demanded her attention as it was the brightest part of that church that was otherwise saturated with mourning people in dark clothing. She focused in on the flag for only a moment, and then looked around at the people surrounding her. There was a lot of crying going on in that church. Too much. She witnessed people wiping tears from their eyes and cheeks, many with tissues in hand, a few just using their bare hands and then wiping them on their shirt or pants. Some just looked down at their laps, faces expressionless.

She didn't want to see sad people. She didn't want to see the casket again either. Searching for something else—anything else—to distract her thoughts, she looked down at the red carpet that covered the aisles of the church. Some of the carpet was frayed where it met the wooden pew. She stared at the frayed part of the carpet for a couple of minutes, just focusing on her breathing. Her chest was rising and falling too quickly. She tried to sit up straight again. She adjusted her posture, pushed her shoulders back a bit. She tried to be present then, because she owed him that, right? But she wanted to be anywhere else in the world. She thought of the sculpture of Jesus outside. He was on a boat, arms out, welcoming her and anyone else around in. That was the point, right? To welcome people out onto the rough seas? Wasn't He supposed to be a source of peace amid troubled waters? Why couldn't she feel that peace now?

Her sadness turned into anger, suddenly. She could feel the heat rising in her cheeks. She was angry at all of them, really. For choosing this job. Why on Earth would you choose a job like this one? For what?

Her eyes drifted to a man a few rows over to her left. She knew he wasn't a cop like the rest. One, because he wasn't in uniform, and every cop there at First United Methodist that day was in their dress uniform. She'd never seen so many cops in one place, actually. And cops from different areas. She looked around and saw NYPD on some uniform patches. Chicago PD. Dallas PD. Lots of cities she wasn't even aware of, some small-town cops. Sheriffs with their big hats. There were even some from out of the country—she'd never seen members of the Canadian Guard in person, and now here they were, in their tall boots and bright red uniform tops, and their funny hats. She couldn't believe how far they had traveled. The other reason she assumed the man to her left wasn't a cop—his beard. Beards were against uniform regulations for most police departments. And it wasn't a manly beard. It was a hipster, skinny-jeans-wearing kind of guy beard. And you know something? She used to judge guys like him, before that day. But looking at him in that moment, she just thought of him as smarter than the rest. He probably had a nice office job or something. Probably no bulletproof vest for him every day. No gun and Taser on his waist. Nope. Probably just wore a nice suit to work and carried a briefcase or something. Smart guy. Not like the people in here.

Her eyes drifted back toward the front of the church. The mayor was speaking now. She only heard bits and pieces of his speech. "There is nothing in the world like the law enforcement world," he said. "No other job will give you as much, or sometimes, take as much. Sometimes it demands the ultimate sacrifice, and today we honor this hero who gave his all . . ."

Her eyes wandered toward the casket again though she tried to avoid it. She didn't want to imagine his body in there. She just couldn't. She looked down at her black ballerina flats. Her chest began to rise again as her breaths became heavier. A lump formed in her throat and her eyes began to sting with tears. Oh, no. No. Not now. You're not going to break down now, she thought. She wanted desperately to distract her thoughts. She looked down again at the place where the red carpet was frayed. She looked up again, and then looked back over at hipster guy a few rows over. Even he was crying.

She thought briefly of escaping. Of going outside, just for a little while. Of walking out to the bronze Jesus sculpture and just standing in the light rain that was falling. The mayor finished his speech, and she watched as the Chief of Police made his way to the podium. It was his turn to speak.

The Chief began by addressing the lifeless man's family first, of course. As he spoke, his eyes were directly on the new widow. His voice cracked as he said, "We are feeling your loss. Your hurt is *our* hurt." Those words made her shake her head. She was sure he meant well, but . . . no. Not exactly the same hurt. The Chief wasn't missing his spouse all of a sudden. But she couldn't help but feel a little sympathy for the Chief too. His face was different then. Every other time she had watched him speak—on the news at press conferences and such—he looked proud. He always came across as strong, well-spoken, and intelligent. He had a chiseled jaw line, patches of gray in his hair—he looked like he could be a man who ran a multimillion-dollar company or something. Not a police department. But then in that church—his face—it seemed to have aged suddenly. It was sorrow that she saw in his face that day at that funeral. Authentic sorrow. It had to be difficult, losing an officer under your authority. She hadn't thought of how this had to affect him yet, not until this moment, as he was up there speaking at that podium. Her eyes drifted back to that dead officer's wife, who was her friend. And to the kids. She couldn't see any of their faces, and was glad for that. But she could hear in her mind their laughter, the last time they were all together. The last time she saw him, too—the man in the casket. He was playing with his kids, chasing them, tickling them. In her memory their laughs were a loud shrieking sound, their faces red. She hurt for them now. Her heart ached. She wondered when they would get to laugh like that again. *If* they would ever laugh like that again. How were they supposed to move forward now? Did anyone have the answer to that?

The Chief continued on and addressed the officers in the room. She was still in disbelief over the number of cops from all over the country there. It was unlike anything she had ever seen. The Chief was taking long pauses in between his words. "Here we are, wearing this uniform," he said. "One family . . . though different, we share a common ground unlike any other. We all chose this job, this life . . . It's hard. It can be *really* hard . . . We know we have a tremendous responsibility to this community and to each other. We know the risks we take. And why do we do this?"

Yes, please answer that one, Chief. Wondering that one myself. She stopped daydreaming about going outside and standing by the sculpture. She studied his face, waiting for what he would say next.

He seemed to adjust his posture then, and stand straighter. He raised his eyebrows. "Because we are willing and able," he said, sternly. "We know this is a calling. And we answer it. Every one of us does. And there is a satisfaction that comes with that."

She nodded. Yes, a calling. Her husband had called it such. What he was saying, it made sense. But despite that, this all still felt senseless. How was that so?

She wished for everything to be different. She wanted so badly for this moment to be a nightmare that she would wake from at any minute. She wanted him out of that damn oak box, alive. She wanted her husband's shift to be happy again, and she wanted her friend to have her husband back. Now her friend was a widow. She was sad for that. When she thought of the word *widow,* she always imagined older women. Not women this age, with young children. It wasn't right.

And the children . . . now they would go through life without their dad. She took a deep breath. She swallowed hard, feeling that lump in her throat again. She shed a tear for those kids, now fatherless.

Her husband looked back at her then. He was sitting with the rest of his shift, the Bravo 400s, not with her. That was the way it was; she didn't take offense to it. Normally spouses didn't even attend funerals. Unwritten rule. They weren't supposed to see this, to think of this as a real possibility even though of course it always was. But she had insisted on being there. So she came and sat a few rows behind her husband and his shift. She noticed the tears in his eyes as he looked back at her. It felt like another prick to the heart, seeing the sadness on her husband's face. He had lost more than a coworker. He had lost a man he called brother. *It could have been him. I could be up there like her. I could be a widow too. But I'm not. Why is that? Why her? It could be us next. Any of us. This job . . . it's too much.*

She looked back up to the front of the church. The Chief was still speaking. "We mourn our brother today, but we also celebrate a man who answered his call and died a true hero," he said. His face was almost brighter then. He spoke matter-of-factly as he looked toward the flag-draped coffin and finished with "We will forever remember you. Blessed are the peacemakers . . . for they shall be called children of God."

With that, the Chief looked away from the coffin and back to the crowd in front of him, and walked away from the podium.

The funeral would be over soon. She panicked a bit . . . she wasn't prepared. She thought at first that she wanted to hurry and have it all be over with. But she knew that it meant he was going into the ground soon. She'd have to accept that he really was in that casket, and he really was dead. She closed her eyes, and for the first time since she could remember, she prayed.

CHAPTER 2

6 MONTHS EARLIER

THE BRAVO 400'S SHIFT was having a Christmas party in a couple of weeks. The Morgan family was hosting by default; originally Chris and Kristin Janacek were hosting. But Kristin's dad had passed unexpectedly after a heart attack, so Chris called Brandon and asked if they could take over the hosting duties.

"We'll be back in town from the funeral," he said. "But Kristin has had even more on her plate with her dad's passing. She helped plan the funeral and all. I want to try and give her somewhat of a break. Can we just move the shift party to your house, Morgan? I'd really appreciate it."

Brandon said yes, of course they would take over, and Leah was glad to oblige. She was close to her dad and couldn't imagine losing him all of a sudden like that. She felt terrible for Kristin.

"Will they still be attending the party?" Leah asked her husband after he ended the phone call with Chris.

"Yeah, I think so," Brandon answered. "Janacek just said that she just didn't want the added work of planning a party in their home right now. And you know, she's already busy with the kids, and now she's grieving on top of that."

"Of course," Leah said. Kristin was already busy, she knew that was true. The Janaceks had five children. Leah and Brandon were newly pregnant with their third, and that felt busy enough.

"Janacek said he already has a lot of decorations, and he is dropping them off at the substation later," Brandon said. "So we just need to buy the food. But people are pitching in money for that, so no big deal."

"Of course," Leah said.

Brandon leaned in to kiss her. She embraced him and felt the Kevlar under his uniform.

"Grace, Ruby, come down and tell Daddy goodbye," Leah yelled up the stairs.

Five-year-old Grace walked down first, wearing a purple princess dress from Halloween and rain boots. Three-year-old Ruby followed shortly after. She was in nothing but undies and was carrying two naked Barbies in her hands. The sight of the attire choices made Brandon smile. "Goodbye, my goofy girls," he said. "I'm off to work."

"Bye, Daddy!" Grace yelled, running up to hug him.

"Yeah, bye, Dad!" Ruby said next. They took their turns hugging and kissing their dad.

"Be good for Mommy," he told them.

"Be safe," Leah said to her husband as he was grabbing his car keys with one hand and slinging his gun belt over his shoulder with the other.

"Always," he said back with a smile. "Love you."

"Love you too."

And with that, Brandon went off to work. He would begin his evening patrol shift and Leah would begin her shift of solo-parenting her two small children at night.

The phone rang shortly after he walked out the door.

Leah answered. "Hello?"

"Leah, hey, it's Cassie," she heard on the other end of the line.

"Hi, Cassie, how are you?" she asked.

"I'm well, thanks," Cassie said. "I heard about Kristin's dad. Awful. I feel just terrible."

"Oh yes, I know," Leah said. "It's very sad. We should send her some sympathy flowers, at the least."

"For sure, absolutely," Cassie said. "And I also wanted to know if you needed any help. I heard the shift Christmas party moved to your house. Do you need me to do anything?"

Leah shook her head as if Cassie could see her. "No, thank you, Cassie, for offering, but we don't have too much to take on," she said. "It's very sweet of you to offer, though."

"Of course," Cassie said. "Well, I should get going. But please call me if you need anything. And hey, I'll send a group email out about getting all of the shift wives to pitch in for a nice flower arrangement for Kristin."

"That sounds good," Leah said. "Bye, Cassie. Talk to you soon."

"Yes, soon," Cassie said. "Good-bye."

Leah hung up the phone and pulled thawed chicken out of a package to bake for her and the girls. She wished Brandon would be home tonight, eating with them. He'd been on this evening shift for forever, it seemed ... but she still had never adjusted to having dinner across from his empty chair at the table.

"Temporary," she said aloud to herself, sprinkling seasoning on the chicken breasts. "One day he will be with us every night."

They had talked of him promoting, of getting a detective job and working regular 9–5 hours. He would be eligible to test and possibly promote soon and this made Leah hopeful, especially because their family was growing.

As she started to peel the potatoes, she heard little footsteps come down the stairs. Grace. She had changed into a swimsuit.

"Little cold for the pool, don't you think?" she asked her oldest child, smiling.

"Me and Ruby are just pretending, Mommy," she said, matter-of-factly. "Hey, are you cooking?"

Before Leah could answer, Grace's shadow, Ruby, came flying downstairs. She was also in a swimsuit.

"Mommy, Mommy, guess what!" Ruby yelled.

"What is it, Ruby?" Leah asked.

"We are swimming away from sharks that live in our room!"

"Wow, Rube," Leah said. "That is really interesting. Okay, you two. You can help me. We are going to get some chicken ready for dinner."

"Yay!" Grace said. She ran and pulled two aprons out. She handed one to Ruby and then pushed a kitchen chair to the island. The two girls stood on the same chair, swimsuits and aprons on, eager to receive instructions from their mother. Leah set a bowl between the two of them and gave them both crackers. "You both crush these with your hands. Put them in the bowl. Got it?"

"Got it!" they said in unison. She snapped a picture of her girls with her phone. She texted it to Brandon and smiled as she hit send. The girls were busy smashing crackers as she mixed parmesan cheese, oregano, paprika, and pepper in another bowl. She set it aside. After she mixed milk and an egg in a third bowl Ruby hopped down from the chair and ran over to her. "Mommy, Mommy, I want to help with this part now! I love using a WIS!"

"It's *whisk*, Ruby, *whisk*," she said, over-enunciating the k. "And sure. Carefully we can use the whisk together."

She held her three-year-old daughter's hand in hers as they whisked the mixture of egg and milk together. Ruby lost interest quickly, however, and went back over to Grace and the crackers.

"Okay, girls," Leah said. "Help me coat this chicken and we can get it in the oven."

After it was in and the timer was set Leah started to clean up the mess. "Clean up, clean up, everybody, everywhere," she sang as she started to wash mixing bowls.

"Mom, is Daddy going to be home for dinner tonight?" Grace asked.

"No, sweetie, he's working," Leah answered.

"Being a peace man?" Ruby asked in her little voice.

"Policeman, Rube. Yes. He is being a policeman."

"I want to be a peace man too!" she said.

Grace chimed in. "Ruby, you are a girl. So you could be a police girl. Not a police man. But I think we should be chefs. Come on, let's go back to the sharks!"

They ran back upstairs and Leah was glad to get another couple of minutes of quiet in her kitchen. Her phone beeped. Brandon had texted back. "Adorable. Love them and love you," the text read.

She sent him a text back. "We love you too."

***

CASSIE HUNG UP THE PHONE after speaking with Leah, and her oldest two walked in the door from school the next minute. They ran into the kitchen and threw their backpacks on the table. She was writing a note to herself on the dry erase board attached to her fridge: "Flowers for Kristin Janacek."

"I'm starved, Mom," Jacob said.

"Dinner isn't until six, kid," Cassie said. She put the dry erase marker away and kissed his forehead. "You can grab a banana or an apple for a snack. Then I need you to get your homework started."

She walked over to her only daughter and kissed her forehead as well. "How was school?"

"Fine," Mackenzie answered. "Except for the bus."

Before Cassie could ask why the bus wasn't fine, the newly turned five-year-old, Noah, came out from in front of *Teenage Mutant Ninja Turtles* to see that his siblings were home. "I thought I heard you, Jacob," he said. "And I'm starving too, Mom!"

"Fine. Grab a quick snack. One. Only one. Get a piece of fruit and that's it. I don't want you spoiling your dinner. Mack, what happened on the bus?"

Mackenzie then leaned forward and vomited, right there on the kitchen floor that Cassie had mopped the previous day.

"Mack, you have to do that in the toilet," Jacob said. "Gross!"

Cassie rushed to get towels to clean the mess, and then washed Mackenzie's face. She handed her a mixing bowl. "Go lie down. If you feel this way again and can't make it into the bathroom, throw up in this bowl. Is this the first time you've thrown up today?"

"Yes, Mom—I'm sorry," Mackenzie said. "I was going to tell you that I felt really sick on the bus and that's why it wasn't fine."

Cassie kissed Mackenzie's head again. "I know you didn't mean to do that in the kitchen, kiddo. I'm sorry you're feeling bad. Go rest, I'll check on you soon."

"Okay, Mom," Mackenzie said, walking to the living room, mixing bowl in her hands. She plopped down on the couch.

Cassie yearned for her husband to be home. He had left for work right before the phone call to Leah. Cassie knew that because the eight-year-old was sick, the other two were sure to follow. She didn't have the energy for sick kids, not today. She and Corey had been arguing too much lately, all over silly things. She knew the agitation she had been feeling toward Corey was attributed directly to her stress. She had been struggling with all she had volunteered to do for the Christmas program at the kids' school, as well as the normal Christmas prep that went into having three children. But that was Cassie, always biting off more than she really wanted to chew.

She threw away a banana peel her five-year-old had conveniently left on the table for her. "Noah, trash can next time," she said to him as she sat down by Jacob to help him get his homework started. "You've got this, son. You can do this math easily. I'll look at it when you're done," she said, leaving the table and gathering the Lysol and Clorox wipes from under the sink. She started spraying Lysol everywhere. The sound of little feet running stopped her. Mackenzie was sprinting to the bathroom. Cassie ran to the bathroom too, and she grimaced as she watched her baby girl violently throwing up in the toilet. She grabbed a ponytail holder and put Mackenzie's hair back. "Mommy's here, sweet girl," she said. She gently put her hand on her daughter's back. She wished she could take her daughter's place in that moment, and take the sickness away.

The vomiting finally came to an end. Cassie gently washed Mackenzie's face and hands and walked her back to the loveseat. "Try and rest, Mack," she said.

She walked back to her boys, still sitting at the kitchen table. Her phone beeped. Text message from Corey. "Sick at work. Still at the sub. As soon as I can get off the toilet will be coming home. Told Sarge already."

Cassie sent him a reply. "Sorry babe. Mack is sick too. See you when you get here. Love you."

She sat in a kitchen chair and put her face in her hands. It would be a long night. She took a deep breath as she mentally prepared for what she imagined her night would consist of. More vomiting, for sure. But as long as she didn't get the bug, she could take care of her family. *I don't have time for this,* she thought to herself.

Corey walked through the door an hour later. Cassie could see right away that he was sick because of how pale his face was. All of the things they had been fighting over the last week, none of it mattered now. She helped him undress from his uniform without saying a word. She had basketball shorts ready for him to change into.

"You take such good care of me, Cassie," her husband said.

"Glad to do it," she said. And she meant those words.

She handed him a cold Gatorade. "Go lie down. Rest. It's a direct order." She smiled at him and he gave a tired smile back. He joined Mackenzie in the living room.

"We're the unlucky ones today, Mack," he said. She didn't respond. He looked closer at her and saw that she was fast asleep, curled up on the loveseat. He hoped he could sleep soon too. He tried to get comfortable on the couch and closed his eyes. Cassie brought him a blanket and kissed his sweaty forehead. When Corey was sick, it was as if Cassie had a fourth child to care for, but she didn't care. She liked catering to her husband.

Cassie heard her phone ring. She left her sick husband and daughter in the living room and returned to the kitchen where her phone was. She saw that it was her mother, Janice.

"Hello?" she answered.

"Hi, Cassandra," Janice said. She was the only person on the planet who called her that.

"Hi, Mama," Cassie replied. "How are you?"

"I'm fine. Calling to ask for my grandbabies this weekend. Can I pick them up on Friday? I've been dying to have them come over, and it would give you and Corey a nice little break."

"Mama, I wish," Cassie said. "There is a stomach bug in my house. Mackenzie was just throwing up, and now Corey is home from work because he's sick too."

"Oh, dear. I'm sorry to hear that. I know it must be bad if Corey is home sick. That man never takes off of work."

"Yeah. He is pretty miserable. I feel bad for him."

"Of course," her mom said. "Well, I am going on a store run anyhow so I'll pick you up a few things and drop them at your door. Crackers, soup. That sort of thing. What else do you need, dear?"

"Oh, Mom, you don't have to do that," Cassie said.

"Shush. I know I don't have to. I want to."

"Okay. What you mentioned sounds great. I could use some Lysol too, I'm about to run out. Thank you, Mama."

They ended the call. The evening went by quickly as Cassie was busy feeding her well children dinner and giving them baths while simultaneously caring for her sick husband and daughter. It hadn't hit anyone else yet. She was glad for that.

She walked over to Mackenzie and saw she was still sleeping. Good, she thought. She needs to sleep this bug off. Then she walked over to her husband.

"I love you, Cassie," he said as she adjusted her blanket to cover him.

"I love you too."

"It's our first date again," he said. "I have déjà vu. And you haven't aged a day."

"Ha. I have absolutely aged, thanks to your children."

Corey had gotten sick on his very first date with Cassie, years before. He always explained while telling the story that he felt sick before he picked her up, but he was afraid that if he canceled the date, he wouldn't have another chance with her. So he went anyway. "I thought I could mind-over-matter the situation," he would say. "Turns out you can't." He had to sprint to the restaurant bathroom before appetizers were served. Cassie wasn't even sure yet if she really liked Corey or not. But that first date, she drove him in his truck back to his apartment and took care of him. It was the vulnerability in him that night that actually attracted her to him. He wasn't proud or arrogant, like the guys she dated before him. Cassie was basically a nurse to him that first night. He asked her, as she was taking his temperature and tucking him into bed, "How is it that you are such a natural at this care-giving stuff? You'll make a great mom one day." It should have been weird, hearing that on a first date. But what was really weird, was that it wasn't. That first night, despite being the complete opposite of romantic, had led to their lives now. They were a family. And it all started with a stomach bug on a first date.

The first date reminiscing ended at the sound of heaving. Cassie quickly looked over at Mackenzie. Wasn't her, she was still asleep. Then Cassie turned toward the kitchen and found the sound. Noah was throwing up on the tile floor.

"Oh, no," Corey said.

Cassie shook her head and headed over to him. "Eh, better than the carpet, I suppose. It's okay, buddy." She rubbed his back. "Mom is here." He finished and she cleaned him up. She made him a pallet of blankets on the living room floor and gave him a mixing bowl. "You know the drill, bud. If you can't make it into the bathroom you throw up here."

His little voice replied, "I know, Mommy."

Cassie turned the television on to Disney Junior and got started on the mess in the kitchen. Whew. Another one down. It would be a long night. She heard a knock at the door. Her mother. She went to open and her mom handed over a couple of grocery sacks.

"Hope this helps a little," she said. "I can stay and help you too, you know."

"Mom, you're the best," Cassie replied. "I don't want to spread germs to you though. You bringing this by, it helps a lot. Noah just started throwing up too."

"Oh, dear. In that case I'm really glad I brought this extra thing for you too."

She pulled a bottle of wine out from behind her back. Cassie smiled and hugged her mom.

"Love you so much," she said.

"Love you too, Cassandra."

She waved as she watched her mom get into her burgundy Toyota Avalon and drive away. *Thank you, Lord, for a wonderful mother who lives five minutes away,* she thought as she watched the car turn off of her street. Back inside the house it was quiet. Eerily quiet. Jacob had opted for video games in his room. For the time being, all three of her sickies were sleeping. Cassie poured a glass of pinot and settled in a chair at the kitchen table with a book. The wine quickly allowed some of the stress she was experiencing to melt away. She would survive her long night.

CHAPTER 3

"WITH HAYES OUT SICK we're down by three now, four counting the rookie," Corporal Harris told Sergeant Torres shortly after Corey left work sick. "White called in again today. Jackson is on vacation. Perales left town for his grandfather's funeral. And now Hayes."

"No problem," Sergeant replied. "I'll call LT, get an approval for an overtime guy. Man. Hayes looked like hell. I'm glad he went home. I don't want to catch that crap."

"Yeah, me neither," Corporal said.

Sarge made the call to the lieutenant from the substation. As soon as he hung up the phone, he heard his call number come through the radio traffic.

"Your presence is being requested for a complaint on an officer."

It was Joe Zavala who was calling on the radio, a senior officer on the shift. He and Chris Janacek, also a senior officer, were on an assault call.

"Ten-four, en route," Sarge said.

"I seriously never have to go on calls with Janacek or Zavala," he said to Corporal Harris. "All of Corpus Christi loves both of those guys."

"I have a text, actually," Corporal said as he was looking down at his phone. "A woman has a complaint to make and asked for a supervisor. Zavala pissed someone off. An older woman, it seems. Should be interesting."

"Zavala never pisses anyone off," Sarge said. "But okay."

The Sergeant drove to the call and arrived at the apartment complex where Zavala and Janacek had taken a call together. A sixty-something-year-old woman in a faded emerald-colored velvet nightgown approached him right away. Zavala was standing shortly behind her. Janacek was busy handing out stickers to the kids at the complex basketball court.

"Oh good," the woman said as she made her way to Sergeant Torres. "You must be the one in charge. Good. I have a complaint. Your officer here, Mr. Zavala, is lazy and I think it needs to be brought to your attention!" she said.

"Well, ma'am, you certainly have my attention," he said. "Please go on."

Zavala looked on and had a smile on his face. He knew Sarge had his back. He also knew he was in the right anyhow, and this complaint had no merit.

"My neighbor slapped me, Officer. Slapped me here on my face." She pointed to her left cheek. "See? Do you see a mark?"

Sarge studied her face. His eyebrows lowered as he leaned in a bit closer. He couldn't see a thing, but was legitimately trying.

"Well, maybe you can't see a mark," she said. "I guess it has faded a little bit. But it's there. It is. And trust me, it is hurt."

"Sorry to hear that, ma'am," he told her. "Do you need medical attention?"

"No. I do not need medical attention. Officer Zavala already asked me that and I told him no. I am just upset that it happened. I believe that you should arrest the woman who slapped me, it is only fair," she said. "And reprimand your officer here, who should have arrested her the first time I asked."

"I understand, ma'am, that you have no family relation to her, is that correct? And she isn't actually here anymore, is that also correct?"

"Thank the Lord we aren't related," she answered. "And she isn't here, of course not. She hit me and ran. But I know you can find her at the Laundromat. Her name is Imogene. She's mean, and ugly. She'll be easy to find."

"All right. I understand you are upset and I would certainly be upset if I were slapped too. However, unfortunately, the law doesn't allow for us to arrest her. Now, if my officer had witnessed her hitting you or if we had some other type of proof, this would be different. But in your case, ma'am, all the law will allow is for us to take a report, and I assure you that Officer Zavala will write a detailed report of what you're telling us."

She crossed her arms across her chest and put her head down. She sighed loudly. Sarge and Zavala watched her, awaiting what they assumed would be more complaining. To their surprise she just said quietly, "Okay then."

"Okay," Sarge said to her. "I will be on my way. I do sincerely hope your day gets better, ma'am."

With that he turned to leave and Zavala started again taking notes for his report. He looked over at Janacek, who was still talking to kids at the basketball court. Once Janacek noticed his Sergeant was there he told the boys goodbye, giving out high fives, and walked over to him.

"So the lady wanted to complain on him, but not on you? What's up with that?" Sarge asked.

"She likes me because I was nice to her grandsons," Janacek said. "I was with them and their friends on the court."

Sarge just nodded and looked over at the basketball court. "Well, I'm out of here unless you need anything else," he said.

"We're good, Sarge. Thank you."

***

ZAVALA AND JANACEK DROVE to a nearby church parking lot to park and finish the report. Zavala started snacking on a bag of mini frosted donuts he had bought earlier from a 7-Eleven.

"Want some?" he asked Janacek.

"I do," Chris answered. He smiled as he enjoyed a donut. "These things are going to kill us."

"Nah, man," Joe said with a full mouth. "Just run it off later, dude. No worries."

He then started swaying his head back and forth and dancing with his shoulders, bouncing them up and down, up and down. Chris looked at him, tilting his head to the side, squinting his eyes.

"There's no music, Zavala," he said.

"In my head, there is always music," Joe said. "And besides, today I am especially excited, bro. Gloria texted me while we were on that call. She said she booked us a surprise trip. Yeah, bro. One-year anniversary is happening next month. I'll be drunk and loving on my bride for days, man. I just don't know where yet. The location is a surprise. She set it up."

"Ah, one year already," Chris said. "Congrats, brother."

"Yeah, thanks, Janacek. For me, third time is the charm. Gloria has it all, bro. But you know what I mean, man. You're a happily married man too."

And he was. Chris Janacek was married to Kristin, his wife of thirteen years and mother of their five children. All aged ten and under. Kristin was a former teacher turned stay-at-home mother and had chosen homeschool for their brood, so she was still teaching but in a different way now. They had busy lives. Happy, busy lives.

"Yes, I do know what you mean," Chris said.

"How is Kristin, by the way?" Joe asked.

"She's okay. She's not been herself exactly since her dad died. But she's strong, and she has a lot of faith, and she is hanging in there. The kids keep her busy. And make her pull her hair out sometimes, you know."

"Ha. I hear that, bro. I remember when mine was young. He's twenty-four now, man. Twenty-four."

"You had him young, huh?" Chris asked.

"Yeah. Early Corps days I met a girl at my first duty station in Cali," Zavala said. "Thought I was in love, you know. But we were too young and too stupid to make that commitment. His mama isn't a bad lady and we stayed married until Joe Junior was two but there was no way it was gonna last past that. So we divorced. Worked out a custody agreement. No drama, really. She remarried. My son has half-brothers. And now me, I have my Gloria. It's all good."

"There was a wife in between your son's mother and Gloria though, right? You said the third time is the charm."

"Yeah, I don't talk about wife number two. Wife two was ten-ninety-six, man. For real. Ten years of hell on earth, bro. Meanest woman I've ever known. I don't know how I stayed married to her for as long as I did. But those days are long gone behind me, man. Gloria is my present and my future, and that is why music plays in my head now."

He started swaying again as he worked on the report and snacked on donuts.

Chris smiled at Joe. He had only met Gloria once, but knew she and Joe were two peas in a pod. They both had big voices, big smiles, and great big laughs. They both had energy that attracted others to them. They seemed as though they had been married for a lot longer than just one year. Chris was happy for Joe. He knew that a good, supportive spouse was a blessing for these guys.

Janacek's cell phone rang. "Speaking of wives . . ." he said, looking down at his iPhone.

"Hey, honey," he answered. "Yeah . . . No, not right now. I can talk. Sitting in a parking lot with Zavala . . . Sure. Zavala, Kristin says hi."

Joe leaned in so Kristin could hear him. "Hi, Kristin," he shouted into the receiver.

"Okay," Chris said. "Yes, I can do that. I'll run it by Sarge but I don't think it will be a problem. Monday evening? Sure. Okay. Love you too. Of course I will. Bye."

Joe looked at Chris with a curious smirk.

"She said hi back. And she wants me to request off on Monday night. Rose has a dance program with the rec center."

"Sweet, man," Joe said. "Rose—she's the littlest girl, right?"

"Yes, she's my youngest daughter. Four years old."

Joe nodded. He wrote more down for his report. A couple of minutes passed.

"Hey, how do you and Kristin seem so happy all the time, with the stress of kids, and this job and all?"

Chris shrugged his shoulders. "We work at it, man," he answered.

"Yeah, I get that," Joe said. "But five kids, that's hard, right? And these hours too. This gig. Kristin is just a rock star, huh?"

"You have no idea," Chris said. He was quiet for a moment. "She's too good for me. I was different before. A screw-up, really. She stuck with me though."

"You, a screw-up? The most straight-laced dude I know? Come on, man. I don't believe that," Joe said.

"It's true. I grew up in this strict household and my parents meant well I'm sure, but all the rules just drove me away. We were at daily Mass every morning. I was homeschooled. But not like my kids are. My mother never smiled at us. She was crazy strict and crazy Catholic. I didn't get to play sports like I wanted. The only thing I ever did outside of the house was altar serve, because my parents made me."

Joe nodded, but didn't say anything. So Chris continued.

"Anyway, it made me want to pull away from the church. I went to college and stopped going to Mass all together. I told myself I would never enter a church again, that I was free from all of that. I started partying. I almost didn't even graduate. But I did. I met Kristin at school . . . When she met me I called myself an atheist."

"You, atheist? There's no way, Janacek. You're kidding me."

"Not kidding. Yeah. She dated me anyways. I think she saw right through me from the start. She knew I was just lost."

"Wow, man," Joe said.

"Yeah. So anyway we started dating. And I cared for her from the beginning, but like I said, I was a big screw-up. I cheated on her. Broke her heart."

Joe's eyes widened. He hadn't known this history that Chris was sharing.

"I'm ashamed. But it is what it is. We broke up for a while. But one day, out of the blue, I'm walking by the campus chapel, which I *always* had to walk by for my last class of the day, and I decided to go inside. I didn't know why. I just felt like I had to go in. So I did. And Kristin was there, kneeling, praying. She didn't notice me at first. I slid in a pew behind her, quietly. Took a few minutes and then she turned around and saw me. She started crying. She said she had been praying for me. I asked her if she had prayed for us to get back together, and she said no. She prayed for me to get back to God."

"Wow," Joe said again.

Chris smiled. "Her prayer was answered. I started to believe again. I started to pray again. I went back to Mass regularly. I remembered the peace only Jesus can give. And I've never looked back. We got back together, obviously. And she's been it for me ever since. We have our ups and downs like every couple. But we both put God first and I know that's what really holds us together."

"Dude," Joe said. "You should be a preacher, man. Oh. Wait. Catholic priests aren't married, are they. Well, you know what I mean, man. You're motivating. You make me want to break out my bible, man. You're good."

Chris shook his head. "Ha. Nah, I just have faith, man. But breaking out your bible isn't a terrible idea."

"Why don't we ride together more often, man?" Joe asked.

"Because I have to ride with Perales normally, remember? I'm his FTO."

"Ah," Joe said. "That's right. Why is he gone, again? I know I didn't get any vacation when I was a rook."

"A few days, I think," Chris said. "And it's not vacation, man. His grandfather passed away. He said he didn't know him all that well, but wanted to pay his respects."

"Oh. Okay. Didn't know that," Joe said. "Is Perales going or staying on our shift once he is off FTO?"

"Sarge said he is staying," Janacek said. "He likes him. I do too, man. He's a good fit with us."

"Yeah, I can see that too. Seems like a good kid."

"He's a hard worker. Funny thing—couple of weeks ago we're on this burglary call. A&M student had her car broken into in the HEB parking lot. Whole call, she's staring at Perales hard core, man. Like—she isn't even trying to hide the fact that she's into him. And she's cute. And the kid is single, man. Does nothing but hang out with his dog after work. He mentioned off to the side to me that he thought she was pretty. So I'm like, dude, ask for her number. And he tells me he's not going to break policy. Ha! I was like, come on, rookie, I'm your FTO and I'm telling you it's not a huge deal. Rook wouldn't budge. Poor girl is probably still wondering why he was acting so disinterested in her."

"Rook, ahhh, being all better than us already," Joe said.

"Ha. Yeah. Better guy than us. I'm glad, like I said, that he is staying on our shift."

Joe nodded in agreement. "Dude. We've been milking this call for too long. Time to go ten-eight."

"Yeah. Let's go."

CHAPTER 4

THE DAY OF THE SHIFT CHRISTMAS party arrived, and Leah was feeling especially nauseous. She was eight weeks into her pregnancy with baby number three, and feeling like vomiting any time she did anything. Sat up too quickly, wanted to vomit. Sat down too quickly, wanted to vomit. Turned her head around to listen to a child, wanted to vomit. Any movement at all, she felt like she was going to lose everything in her stomach. She tried to push through it, but was miserable.

"I'm sorry to put so much of this on you," she told Brandon as he was setting out the last of the appetizers on their dining room table.

"Babe, you're sick. I don't mind."

"Thank you, Brandon," she said as she kissed his cheek.

She walked to the kitchen, slowly, to grab saltines and ginger ale. She looked at the counter and focused in on the two bottles of whiskey and the bottle of pinot noir. She realized that keeping this pregnancy from the shift may be difficult. For one, she had to try and hide her nausea, which she wasn't so sure she could do. And two, she wouldn't be drinking, which would raise a flag for a few of the ladies. She and Cassie always drank pinot together at shift get-togethers; it had become their thing.

She sighed at the thought of continuing to keep this from Cassie. *Maybe I'll just tell her,* she thought. *No, no. I need to wait. Till twelve weeks at least. Till the safe zone.* Her heart stung a bit in that moment as she remembered a time she hadn't waited to tell people. A pregnancy in between Grace and Ruby. She told everyone she was pregnant the day after she had seen two pink lines on the stick. She was ecstatic. She and Brandon had always wanted kids close in age, and their dream was coming true. But six weeks in, and the very day after she had told everyone, she lost the baby. It was hard enough to go to that six-week checkup and hear that her baby didn't have a heartbeat, and never would. But it made it harder to have to tell everyone that—never mind—we aren't having another baby yet. So now, she would wait. Until the second trimester. Until the safe zone.

Brandon walked into the kitchen then. "I think we're all set for people to show. You going to be okay? Or are you gonna puke in front of everyone?"

"I'm fine. Though puking in front of your shift would be super fun for me."

Leah smiled at her husband, and he winked at her. He grabbed a Shiner Bock out of the fridge. "I'm starting now," he said, using his wedding band to pop the top off. And with that, the doorbell rang. "Party time," he said.

Alex Mang was the first to arrive, exactly six minutes until the actual party start time. "Of course, Mang, you would be the first here," Brandon said, shaking his hand at the front door.

"Am I early?" he replied.

Leah leaned in for a hug. "You're right on time," she said.

"No, he's early," Brandon said. He looked at Alex. "Mofo, you can help me finish cleaning for the party now."

"Don't listen to a word he's saying, Alex, we were ready for guests," Leah said, shaking her head. "And Brandon—LANGUAGE!"

"Our kids are nowhere near the vicinity right now," Brandon said. "We don't have to censor ourselves tonight."

Alex lifted a wrapped shoebox-shaped gift. "Where are we putting these?"

"I'll take it," Leah said, as she walked it to the Christmas tree.

Leah liked Alex Mang. He had a gentle, sweet nature about him. She couldn't imagine him hurting a housefly, and yet, he was the only cop she knew personally who had shot a man. It was a righteous shoot, of course. A senile old man with a death wish took his pump shotgun out to a farmer's market one Saturday morning and randomly shot it into a tree, terrifying the patrons. 911 calls started coming in, one from a ten-year-old boy hiding under a table of jams and jellies, telling the dispatcher his mother was hiding under the table with the peppers and he had her cell phone because he had been playing Angry Birds when he heard a loud bang.

Mang was the first on scene. The old man saw him and pointed his shotgun directly at Mang. Alex yelled out twice, "Drop the gun! Drop the gun!" quickly, loudly. The old man ignored his command and refused to put his gun down, so Alex Mang did what he had hoped that he would never have to do, but what he was trained to do. He fired one round from his pistol, taking the old man to the ground.

Backup arrived at the very moment of the shot. Mang's voice, a bit shaky, called over the radio, "Shots fired. Start EMS. One suspect down." Brandon Morgan and Brian White ran up. Brandon said to Mang, "You good, man?" Mang just replied, "Yes." Nothing more. Brian started CPR on the old man right away as the horrified crowd looked on. EMS showed up shortly after and took over.

The old man survived the shot, initially. Died a week later in the hospital. Mang was placed on administrative leave for a couple of weeks, but the investigation was quick, as it was plain as day that it was a justified shoot. He quickly went back to work and acted as though nothing had occurred at all. Leah believed he probably handled it just fine even behind closed doors. He seemed mentally strong. He was also smart. Really smart. He had planned initially to be a doctor—a surgeon, actually. He would've seen death in a different way in that field, and been able to handle that too. But his heart wasn't in the medical world, he had said. Much to the disappointment of his overbearing parents, who had groomed him his entire life to be a surgeon like his father, he became a cop instead. He said police work was his dream job.

Now he was standing in Leah's house having a Shiner Bock with Brandon, who was still making fun of him for showing up a few minutes early.

Doorbell rang. This time, Chris and Kristin Janacek stood at the doorstep. Kristin's golden blonde hair shone under the glow of the porch light. She looked perfect, as always. Leah wondered often how she had time to do that, with five children at home. Leah felt like most days she could hardly get a shower in, let alone spend time on hair and makeup.

"Welcome," Leah said, leaning in to hug Kristin.

"Leah, thank you for agreeing to host. It was a huge relief to pass this over to you. And the flowers you ladies had sent to our house, they were so beautiful. Thank you so much."

"It was the least we could do," Leah said. "My condolences again, Kristin. I'm really sorry for your loss."

Kristin looked down. "Thank you, Leah. I'm better now than I was when he first passed. My dad had a good life, and he is in Heaven now. I miss him, but try to focus on where he is now. So it's okay. I'm okay."

The ladies smiled at each other again and walked inside. Alex walked up and said hi. The rest of the shift started trickling in. Joe Zavala with his wife, Gloria. They could be heard coming from miles away, they both had such roars for voices. Adrian Rodriguez arrived with his "flavor of the week," as the shift called his girlfriends. This time, a cougar, much older than the twenty-four-year-old Adrian. Robbie Jackson and his wife, Natasha, arrived. Then Corey and Cassie Hayes. Sarge showed up then with his wife, Eva, and the Corporal was right behind him with his wife, Becca. Danny Perales showed up alone, as did the lone female on the shift,

Mandy Jacobs. She had a boyfriend, but he lived in another town. The shift often joked that he was make-believe.

The last to arrive, an hour after the party started, was Brian White. "I don't even care if that douche-bag comes," Brandon said before Brian came through the door. "I hope he stays home."

"Not nice, Brandon," Leah said, playfully smacking his arm.

"Hey, he's not a nice guy," Brandon said. "Not a team player either. I'm not the only one who feels this way."

Robbie Jackson overheard them and chimed in. "White is an arrogant, lazy piece of crap."

Leah's eyebrows rose. If Robbie was adding his two cents in, it was a big deal. Robbie didn't usually contribute to a conversation like this one, not unprovoked. He was an Army Ranger in his past life, and a good-looking one to boot. The shift nicknamed him "Denzel" after a drunk woman he arrested for DUI kept calling him "Officer Denzel Washington" in the patrol car on the way to the city jail. His wife, Natasha, was attractive too. She was also an Army veteran, but now worked for Veterans Affairs. They were childless, but Brandon had mentioned to Leah that Robbie said at one time they were trying and having trouble.

"See?" Brandon said to Leah. "Jackson doesn't like him either. Told ya."

Leah just shook her head, and Brian walked in.

"Speak of the devil," Brandon said.

"You're late," Corey said jokingly, as he walked up to shake Brian's hand. He was the only one on the shift to do so.

"Yeah, sorry about that," Brian said. "I didn't want to come." He had a smirk on his face. Leah knew his reputation, and knew he tended to come off as having an ego he couldn't back up because his work ethic was far from par. But she had also heard that he was divorced and alone, and couldn't help but feel like maybe that had something to do with it. She pitied him.

Leah's thoughts of Brian were quickly interrupted as she felt a nudge on her shoulder. She turned around and Cassie was holding two glasses of pinot noir. She handed one to Leah, who had an awkward reluctant pause.

"Pinot time!" Cassie said with a smile. Upon noticing Leah wasn't as eager as normal, she then said, "Come on, Leah. We all have breaks from our kids tonight. And pinot, it's our drink!"

"Of course," Leah said. In that moment she took a small sip, and decided she could walk around with her glass, occasionally sneaking away to pour some out. No one would notice, and the wine in her hand would surely prevent any speculation of a new pregnancy.

Adrian walked up to Leah and Cassie then, hand in hand with his date. "Ladies, have you met Cynthia yet?" he asked. They gave quick, polite introductions, and then she asked Leah and Cassie, "May I get in on some of that wine?" It would be the only time she would speak to the wives all night. She spent the rest of the evening drinking, laughing too loudly at all of the men's stories, and touching Adrian in borderline inappropriate ways even for a party amongst adults. It would have embarrassed anyone else, but Adrian—he didn't care. He knew Cynthia was temporary in his life, and he also knew that the shift was aware of that as well. His reputation was one of a player and he didn't try to hide that.

"She looks like she's old enough to be his mother," Zavala said to Danny Perales as they snacked together on chips and queso by the dining room table. "He won't be able to handle this one, man. She'll chew him up and spit him out."

"Yeah, dude, but you know Adrian, he'll have someone else by next week regardless," Perales said.

"True, true," Joe said. "And what about you, rook? You play the field like him?"

Danny shook his head. Chris walked up then as he heard them talking and joined the conversation.

"Rook could've had a date here too, but he was being a little girl about it last time I saw him get hit on," Chris said, smiling.

"Oh yeah, rook, heard some chick on a burglary call was digging on you and you dissed her, man," Joe said.

"Ha. Funny you guys should mention that. I saw her again, couple of days ago. For real. She's a barista at the Starbucks next to my apartment complex. Got a coffee on my way into work, and she recognized me."

"So, you finally man up and ask her out, or what?" Chris asked.

Danny nodded yes.

"Wait, what? Ahhhh, no way, rook! Ha ha!" Zavala laughed as he punched Perales in the arm. "Rookie boy has a date, how cute. Dude. You have some balls after all! What a relief. I was starting to think you had a crush on me, bro, and that's why I never see you with any girls. Ha!"

Leah noticed their conversation, and saw the beet red in Danny's cheeks.

"No big deal, guys, just taking her to dinner next weekend," he quietly said. He was smiling but looked embarrassed.

"Leave him alone, bullies," Leah said. "Danny. Pay no attention to these guys."

"Oh, they aren't bothering me, Mrs. Morgan," Danny said. "I'm just being all weird I guess because I actually like this girl, and I just met her. So I guess it's a weird thing for me and still weird to even talk about."

"First of all, it's Leah, not Mrs. Morgan. You should know this by now," Leah said. "And secondly, good for you. What's her name, Danny?"

"Sierra," he answered.

"Pretty name," Leah said.

"Yeah. And she's a pretty girl," he replied. "And she's so funny. We talked on the phone the other day for four hours. Four hours. Unbelievable, right? And she had me laughing so much it hurt. I don't know. It sounds corny probably, but it feels like this could really be something, Mrs. Morgan. I mean, Leah."

Leah smiled at him. She liked Danny. She knew her husband respected him too. Brandon had spoken highly of him when he first started his field training on their shift, and was pleased when it was announced that he would be staying with them.

"Well, Danny, I am happy for you. I hope I get to meet her sometime at one of these shift parties."

Danny nodded. "If all goes well, I'll start bringing her around," he said.

"Let's get white elephant started," Sergeant Torres announced from the other room. As everyone else was migrating to the living room Leah snuck into the kitchen to discreetly pour some wine from her glass to the sink. She felt a little dizzy, which was the norm for her in this first trimester. And the timing was fine. She could sit a while in the living room as everyone played white elephant. She left a tiny sip in her glass and went to sit down on her couch. Brandon winked at her as he got the game started. Couples played as one, so he drew a number for the both of them and she was able to relax as everyone took their turn opening the array of silly gifts.

Joe opened a bottle of diet pills that were gifted along with a pack of Diet Coke. "Hey, somebody tryin' to tell me something?" he said, patting his own stomach.

"Yeah, Zavala, you got to lay off the donuts," Chris answered him. Everyone laughed.

Brian White opened a gift that had a six-pack of non-alcoholic beer in it. "Aw, man, this is garbage," he said.

Danny Perales opened a gift card to Krispy Kreme Doughnuts. "This isn't even a gag gift, y'all, I hit the jackpot," he said, smiling. There was a lot of laughter in the room.

In that moment, Leah was grateful. Grateful for her husband's coworkers, grateful for the babysitters that ensured all parents in attendance could have kid-free time, and grateful also for the new little life inside her that was still hidden from the people she was sharing a room with at the moment. She wanted for nothing. And that felt really good.

Cassie walked over after white elephant ended and grabbed Leah's wine glass. "Looks like you need more!" she said. "I do too. Let's go fill our glasses!"

"Clearly, I'm driving tonight," Corey said. He slapped Cassie's bottom.

"Corey Hayes, you stop that right now," Cassie said, smiling. "Save it for when we're alone."

Corey kissed his tipsy wife as she and Leah continued to walk to the kitchen for more wine. Mandy Jacobs was heading to the kitchen also, talking with Corporal Harris and his wife, Becca. This was Mandy's first time meeting the Corporal's wife. All she knew about her was that they had one child, a boy, and that she was a teacher.

"Do you enjoy teaching?" Mandy asked Becca, hoping to spark a good conversation. Mandy knew that not all officers' wives liked the idea of female cops. Some women were just jealous by nature, and the idea of their husbands working all day with another female—a female who chose work in a male-dominated field—rubbed them the wrong way.

"I do," Becca said with a warm smile. "I have second graders, and I love teaching second grade. This year is especially great, actually, because our Max happens to be in second this year and his current teacher is in the class next door to mine. It's nice having him so close by."

"I'll bet," Mandy said. "You know, I would probably teach if I didn't do this. I come from a family of teachers. My grandmother, my father, my aunt, and my sister all teach."

"Wow, that is a lot of teachers in one family," Becca said. "So, what made you become a cop instead?"

Mandy smiled. "My dad used to watch *CHiPs* when I was little, remember that show?"

Becca nodded.

"It's weird, but I wouldn't watch anything else as a kid—but when that show was on, I would be glued to the television, watching with my dad. He used to joke with my mom that I would grow up and be a policewoman. And I can't explain *why* exactly, but I kind of knew he was right—that I would do this. I just always knew I wanted to. I ended up at Texas State and got my criminal justice degree, and one day CCPD had a recruiter on campus that did a good job selling Corpus to me. And now I'm here, obviously. I love it."

"You love this, Jacobs?" Brian White chimed in. "You sure? I can't tell when you're dodging calls all day."

Corporal looked annoyed. "She does twice the amount of work you do, White," he said.

"Oooohhh, snap!" Zavala said in passing.

White rolled his eyes but it shut him up.

"I do love this job," Mandy said. "Just not all of my coworkers." She was looking directly at Brian as she said it, but he was already walking away.

Kristin and Chris walked up then to Leah and Brandon. "Sorry to bail," Kristin said. "But our sitters tonight happen to be two teenagers who we aren't paying much. We need to get back. But this was fun, really. And a nice distraction from everything going on lately. Thank you both again for hosting. We love you guys."

Kristin and Leah hugged each other. Even Chris and Brandon hugged. "We love you guys, too," Leah said. "As always, it was so great seeing you."

Brian White was the next to leave, but he didn't say anything. He did a quick wave and left.

Everyone started trickling out after that. Cassie and Corey were the last to leave. "My mom is with our kids and she texted me that there is no rush, the kids are all *asleeeep*," Cassie said, slurring her speech as Corey was pushing her out the door.

"These two don't want us here literally all night, Cassie," Corey said.

"You two gotta pick up your kids still, man? Sorry for staying so late. I didn't mean for us to overstay."

Brandon shook his head. "No, man, kids are overnight with Leah's parents tonight," he answered. "You didn't overstay at all."

"See?" Cassie said.

Corey smiled. "My wife hasn't gotten out in a while. And she's a lightweight."

Cassie tripped then on the front porch. Corey was able to grab her right before her face would have met pavement. He shook his head but was laughing.

Brandon shook Corey's free hand. The other was holding Cassie up. "You're good to drive, right, Hayes?"

"I stopped drinking after only one, man. You know you don't have to worry about me. I'll be able to drive home." He looked at his wife and chuckled. "Man, my wife just reminded me of that drunk guy that almost fell into you with his knife last week," Corey said to Brandon.

Brandon's eyebrows rose and then he looked over at Leah, hoping by some miracle she hadn't heard that. "Ha! Yeah, man," he said to Corey. "Be safe getting her home, Hayes. Have a good night. See you at work."

Leah's eyebrows wrinkled in confusion. She waited until Corey and Cassie were in their car to ask Brandon what Corey had been talking about.

"Someone came close to 'falling into you with a knife' last week? You mean you almost got stabbed? I don't remember you ever telling me that. Why wouldn't you tell me that?"

They walked inside and Brandon locked the door.

"Leah, it was a really drunk guy who had a knife, and yes, it was out. But I wasn't hurt. I didn't feel like worrying you with it. It wasn't as bad as it sounds. We had everything under control."

"I thought you told me everything though. I want to know these things."

"Again, Leah. It would have been unnecessary worry. I was just trying to avoid giving you extra stress when I know you already have it tough at home with the kids."

"Brandon, I'm not just some girl you're dating. I'm your wife. I don't want you keeping stuff like that from me. I can't believe you were almost stabbed and I didn't know about it."

"Leah, I know you aren't just some girl. It wasn't my intent to hurt you by keeping this one from you, it was me protecting you from worry. Okay? That's it. But I won't keep any more calls from you, okay?"

Leah had been crossing her arms but she uncrossed them then and fell into Brandon. "I love you, Brandon. I want to know what happens to you at work. Even the really bad stuff."

Brandon kissed his wife's forehead. "All right, Leah. Got it. I'll be better about telling you about my calls. But you have to know that my intentions are good. I want to protect you from extra worries."

He looked down at his watch then. "It's late, what do you say we get some sleep while we can? Kid-free sleep sounds great, right?"

"Right," she said.

Not more than fifteen minutes later, snuggled under their quilt, Leah giggled quietly as Brandon started to snore. Seven years of marriage and she still thought he looked cute as he slept. She closed her eyes, and was quickly able to join him in a deep sleep.

CHAPTER 5

THE BRAVO 400S WORKED on Christmas Eve. Sarge and Corporal walked into show-up wearing Santa hats with bells. The shift could hear the jingles before they actually entered the room.

"Corporal must've given Sarge the hat," Corey said to Chris and Joe, who were sitting with him. They nodded in agreement. It wasn't Sarge's character to be goofing around in a Santa hat. He was usually serious, stoic. Quiet unless he needed to be loud. Never silly, never playful.

"Merry Christmas Eve," Corporal said, throwing out Whataburger gift cards to everyone.

"SWEET!" Zavala said, catching his in the air. "I know where I'm going for seven tonight. Taquitos are callin' my name!"

Corporal then proceeded to read the list of BOLOs to the shift. He was interrupted by Brian White, who walked in late.

"Nice hats, man," White said as he slid into his seat. His arrogant smirk seemed to display his disregard for the time.

"It's nice of you to grace us with your presence, White," Corporal said. He took one last gift card out from his pocket and threw it to him. "A gift from me and Sarge. And hey, White, maybe start trying harder to be on time, eh?" He sighed.

"Yeah, yeah," Brian said. "I was hardly late though, and, I mean, it's Christmas Eve, but whatever."

"If the rest of the shift can be on time, then so can you, White," Sarge said. "It's Christmas Eve for all of us. All right. Let's get to work. And let's try to be off on time, all right? All right."

Chris looked over at Danny. "Ready to ride with me for the last time before you're on your own?"

"Yes, Janacek, I am," Danny replied.

"You've gotta be sick of Janacek by now, Perales," Joe joked. "I bet you wish your last riding day with him was last week. Ha."

"Janacek has been a great FTO, actually. I feel like I've learned a lot from him."

"Aww, rook. You're such a nice guy. I'm just busting Janacek's balls. But look at you, calling him great. You're a good one, rook. Still positive. Couple more weeks and you'll be jaded like the rest of us."

As soon as Chris and Danny were in their patrol car, Danny asked about what Zavala had said. "You think Zavala is right, I'll be jaded soon?"

Chris shrugged. "If you want to call it that, I guess."

"You don't seem jaded, though," Danny said. "I would never describe you as jaded. So why is that?"

"You just can't see it," Chris answered. "I'm different than I was too. I wanted to be a superhero out here, rook. Like you. I was on fire. I wanted to save the world. But . . . hell, man, you start to see things about people the longer you're here. Things you don't want to see. Humans are bizarre, dude. The things people do behind closed doors—to each other, to themselves—society doesn't have a clue about the screwed-up stuff we end up seeing. So yeah. I'm a bit cynical now. But—my faith, my family, they keep me grounded. And I'm good at shutting all of this off when I get home. Or at least, I try. And Kristin says I do a good job of shutting it off."

Danny was listening intently, nodding his head.

Chris started again. "One night I didn't shut if off though. My kids were sleeping, obviously, when I got home from my first traffic fatality. I was so angry. I woke Kristin because I was slamming cabinets looking for liquor. She came in the kitchen and asked me what the heck was wrong with me. A kid died in that crash that night. A kid my oldest at the time's age. Drunk driver. I'd seen dead bodies before, but never a kid. The drunk driver survived. Hardly had a scratch. I was so mad at him, I wanted to kill him. I wanted to hold him down, make him look at that dead little girl, and then shoot him in the face. I really did. So that night, I didn't 'shut it off' when I got home. But Kristin, she poured some whiskey for both of us. She listened to me. She prayed with me. I kissed all of my sleeping kids and went to bed with my wife by my side. I'm blessed by my family, rook. I am. But yeah . . . sometimes I can be a bit jaded too. Because of crap like that."

They were both quiet for a moment.

"Maybe one day I'll have a family too," Danny said. "Maybe sooner than later, even. I hope."

"Oh yeah—the Starbucks girl—how's that going?" Chris asked.

"Sierra, her name is Sierra," Danny said. "It's good, real good. I don't want to jinx anything but I like her a lot. We talk every day."

"Good to hear, buddy," Chris said.

Danny smiled, as it was the first time Janacek had called him that. Normally it was "dude" or "rook." He was becoming a peer, and it felt good.

***

MANDY JACOBS FOUND HERSELF on a call that Christmas Eve night she initially dreaded taking. "Sex Crimes, Urgent," the computer had said. A twenty-year-old girl had called the police and wanted to report something. Mandy tried to prepare herself to be both cop and psychologist as she drove to the call. She'd been on calls before and had to console women who had been sexually assaulted. It was never easy, and she had wanted to take it easy that night.

The girl actually had a big goofy grin on her face as Mandy arrived, which automatically struck Mandy as odd.

"Officer, hi, I'm so glad they sent another woman," the girl said.

"I'm Officer Jacobs, with the Corpus Christi Police Department," Mandy said. "You called to report a sex crime?"

"Oh, yes, Officer Jacobs," she said. "I'm Breanna. I'm a student at A&M Corpus. I want to report a rape."

"Do you need emergency medical services?" Mandy asked, getting ready to call for EMS on her radio.

"Oh no, no, I am totally fine," Breanna replied. Mandy had her notepad out and was writing as Breanna spoke. She didn't need to ask any further questions, because Breanna just started to ramble.

"A couple of weeks ago, I went to a party with some friends. Wasn't looking to meet anyone, but I did. I met a guy named Brett. Really cute guy, and charming, you know? Anyway, one thing led to another, and I had sex with him. He was really laying on the charm and made me think he liked me. Now I feel like I need to report it as a rape, because I think he tricked me. He pretended to like me so that I would have sex with him, and now he doesn't answer my calls. I regret the sex. He tricked me. It was rape."

Mandy looked up at Breanna from her notepad. "Did he force himself on you, or was the sex consensual?" she asked.

"He didn't force it, no."

"So, it was consensual."

Breanna rolled her eyes. "Technically, I guess."

"Did you tell him no at any time during the sex, or ask him to stop at any time?"

"No, no, I didn't."

"Were you inebriated at the time? Had you been drinking, or taken any sort of drug at all?"

"No. I actually wasn't drinking because I had a test the next Monday, and the last time I got that messed up at a party the weekend before a big test, I bombed it big time. So I stayed sober."

Mandy sighed and tried to hide the agitation on her face. "Breanna, did he do anything during sex that you didn't welcome him to do? Was there any point during the sex in which you were not a willing participant?"

"Well, no," Breanna said. "But the point is, Officer, he was *acting* like he liked me to get me to sleep with him. So he *tricked* me."

Mandy stopped writing then. She looked at Breanna dead in the eyes. "That is not rape," she told her.

"But, Officer, I think he tricked me," Breanna said. "Didn't you hear that? Like, he lied and acted like he liked me to get me to sleep with him."

"You told me the sex was consensual, and that he didn't force himself on you, correct?"

"I mean, yeah, he didn't force himself . . ."she said.

"And you were sober, you told me that also, correct?"

"I told you, I didn't drink that night, and I've never done drugs," Breanna said.

"Then what you did was have consensual sex, Breanna," Mandy said. "And what you are doing now is wrong. I've seen real rape, Breanna. I've seen women nearly beaten to death after and hanging on for their lives by a thread. I've seen real victims and you know something? People like YOU make it hard for them to come forward. People like YOU make real victims have a hard time being seen as credible. You should be ASHAMED of yourself, Breanna. Why are you doing this? And on Christmas Eve, for crying out loud. Don't you have somewhere else to be?"

Breanna looked at her with shock. "For your information, I do not celebrate Christmas. Not that it's any of your business. And by the way, I'm going to report this to your supervisor," she said to Mandy then. "You can't talk to me this way."

"I'll call him for you now, if you'd like," Mandy said, starting to tug at her radio to send traffic through to her Sarge.

"No, no, never mind," Breanna said. "Actually I don't want to talk to another officer. Or you. Just leave, Officer. I'm done with you."

Breanna turned around dramatically, flipping her hair a bit, to walk back into her apartment.

Ignorant girl, Mandy thought to herself as she walked to her patrol car. *This is not how I want to be spending my Christmas Eve.*

***

THE FOLLOWING DAY, BRANDON found himself playing the familiar role of referee to his daughters. "Hey, girls, fighting isn't allowed on Christmas," he said, pulling a stuffed bear Ruby and Grace were playing tug of war with.

"But I had it first!" Grace shouted.

They had just walked in from the Christmas service at church. He put the bear on top of the entertainment center in their living room. "Now, neither of you get to play with it. You need to learn to share."

"Not fair!" Ruby said, her lip quivering.

Leah pulled her in for a hug. "I have an idea, Rube," she said. "How about we make hot cocoa."

"With marshmallows?" Ruby asked.

Leah wiped the tears from Ruby's cheeks. "With marshmallows."

"Great idea, Mommy," Brandon said. "I'll get that started. You girls change out of your pretty Christmas dresses so we don't get them dirty."

"Great idea, Daddy," Leah said. She took the girls upstairs and changed them.

Propped on the couch a little while later, comfortable in her flannel snowman pj's, hand over her belly, Leah smiled. Next Christmas they would have another baby here with them. It was a beautiful feeling, one of completeness.

***

ACROSS TOWN, CORPORAL HARRIS wasn't having as stellar of a time with his Christmas Day off, as he argued with his wife.

"This is BS, and you know it, Jared," Becca said. "You're shutting me down without even a conversation first."

She was referring to a conversation she tried to start with Jared that morning. Her father, a bigwig for a lucrative construction company, had a project manager position open up that he wanted to offer to Jared before anyone else. He called and talked to Becca about it, and once she told Jared, he seemed offended and didn't respond.

"Becca, you know I love my job," he said. "Why even ask me? Seriously. And it's Christmas Day, for crying out loud. You have a lot of nerve, Bec. Wow."

Max had been busy playing with a new Lego world that Santa dropped off that morning. Jared and Becca didn't realize he had been listening to them argue until he chimed in unexpectedly.

"Dad, I don't want you to be a policeman either," he said. "Listen to Mom. Go work with Grandpa. Please."

Jared looked down at his son. "What, buddy? I thought that you liked that I am a police officer, Max. Remember that time you came to the substation and I showed you around? Remember how cool you thought the lights and siren were on my patrol car?"

"It's not cool, Dad," Max answered. "I don't think it's cool anymore. You could die, Dad. Did you know that? You could be shot and die. Daddy, construction trucks are cool too. Maybe if you ask Grandpa he'll let you drive a bulldozer. That would be cooler, Daddy. And then you won't die."

Becca and Jared looked at each other quickly, with looks of equal parts surprise and confusion.

"Why do you say that, Max?"

Max looked down and fiddled some more with his Legos. He sighed. "My friend Ethan at school told me. He said he watches the news, and he says that they say that policemen get shot all the time. And they die. Did you know that? Policemen die."

Max then put the Legos down and looked up at his dad. Tears started to well in his eyes.

"Daddy, don't fight with Mommy," he said. "Just say yes and work with Grandpa. Please. I don't want for you to die."

Jared scooped his son up in his arms. "I'm not going to die, Max. Don't you worry about that. And don't listen to Ethan. He's wrong, Max. Okay? Police officers do NOT get shot all the time. Look at me and Daddy's work friends. We've been doing this a long time. And we're okay, aren't we? I'm okay and so are all of my friends. And it's going to stay that way. You got that, Max? I don't want for you to worry. Okay?"

It was quiet for a moment.

Becca, with a look of defeat in her eyes, tried then to console her seven-year-old. She patted his back as he was leaning into his dad's chest. "Dad is right, Max," she said. "Ethan is wrong and I'm sorry he made you worry. Your dad is going to stay safe. And he loves his job, buddy. You won't hear any more arguing from me and him about this. Especially not today. It's Christmas Day, buddy. There's no crying on Christmas Day."

Jared kissed his son's head. Then Becca leaned down and kissed Max too. After, she looked up into Jared's eyes. He gently pecked her lips.

"You know what?" Becca said. "I know what we need to do. We should make popcorn and watch *Polar Express*."

"Great idea," Jared said. "What do you say, Max?"

Max nodded and gave a half smile. "Yeah, I like that movie."

Becca mouthed *I'm sorry* to Jared as they went to the living room to put the movie in. Jared sat Max down on the couch and embraced Becca. "There is no need to apologize," he said. "I'm sorry too. I didn't need to react the way I did when you mentioned it. I love you."

"I love you too," Becca responded. "And I know you love your job. I know that. Sometimes I just think—maybe it would be easier if you did something else. But I don't want to argue, and I want to be supportive of you. So I will be."

"You've always been so supportive, Bec, and I understand you wanting for me to do something else. I know my job isn't easy on you. I do. This is who I am, though, Becca. I don't think I can change it."

"I know," she said. "I know."

CHAPTER 6

"WELCOME BACK TO WORK," Sarge said to the shift. "Hope you all had a good Christmas Day off. We ought to have a couple of good slow days, and then lucky us, we'll be here New Year's Eve and that's always eventful. Let's get to work, but try to be off on time. All right? All right."

Everyone was starting to walk out and get to their patrol cars but Robbie Jackson lingered behind. "Sarge, sir, do you have a couple of minutes?" he asked after it was only the two of them left in the room.

"I do," Sergeant Torres said. "What's going on, Jackson?"

"Sir, I don't mean to bother you with this, but I have a personal question, actually. If it's an okay time."

"It's fine, continue," Sarge said with a curious head tilt.

"I was told you've adopted kids. I don't mean to pry, but I have some questions about how long you waited, if you don't mind me asking."

Sarge lifted his eyebrows. "You and the wife contemplating adoption?"

"Well, sir, we've been heading that way. Natasha and I tried for years to get pregnant and have one of our own, but never did have any success with that. So we moved on. We're both older now, and knew if we wanted children, adoption is the route we'd have to take.

So we did the home study business, and are officially on a wait list. They told us a timeline. But I'm wondering how long it was for you."

Sarge nodded. "Well, Jackson, it's been a long time since we did it, my daughters are nineteen and twenty-one now. If I remember correctly it was about a year and a half to get our first daughter. Second time around was quicker, say six months or so? It's a crapshoot, I think. But good luck to you, Jackson. Keep me posted."

"Will do. Appreciate it, sir."

"No problem. Got anything else for me?"

"No sir, that was it. Thank you, Sarge."

Sergeant Torres stopped Robbie right before he left the room. "Hey, Jackson," he said.

Robbie turned around. "Yes, Sarge?"

"Good for you. Real good." Sarge was nodding his head as he said it.

"Thank you, sir," Robbie said, and he turned back around to get to work.

Later that evening Robbie and Corey were on a call together.

"Lady says there's a prowler in her yard," Corey said to Robbie. "I've been out here a time or two before though. The lady calls for random stuff. Never actually had a real problem out here but she calls anyway. She lives alone and I think she just wants the company."

They began searching around the perimeter of the house with flashlights, hearing nothing, seeing nothing. As they were wrapping up their search a gray, mangy-looking cat came jumping out of the garbage can on the side of the house. "Dang, think that's the prowler?" Robbie said, smiling.

The woman came onto her porch when the officers were finished looking around her property.

"Officers, thank you for coming," she said. "For your service, I have tea and muffins inside. Please, please come in."

Walking into the house, Robbie remembered Corey saying she was lonely, and he could sense that. He noticed that the television was turned to the Game Show Network, but the sound was muted. There were stacks of home and gardening magazines in three separate areas of the living room. There was a knitting needle and two unfinished blankets draped over a rocking chair. The woman had to be in her eighties. No family pictures to be found anywhere.

"Oh, Officers, you are so kind to come," she said, handing each of them a blueberry crumble muffin on a square quilted napkin.

"Happy to do our job, ma'am," Corey said. "I do believe your prowler was just a hungry stray cat."

"Oh, that is right. Silly me. I've seen that ol' cat before. Well, thank you for checking. You officers should stay a while, enjoy your muffins. Your tea is almost ready. What are your names, Officers?"

"I'm Officer Robbie Jackson, ma'am, and this here is Officer Corey Hayes."

"Corpus Christi's finest," she said. "I've lived here for thirty years, and you two are just the most handsome officers I've met." She smiled. "I moved here from San Antonio after my husband passed on. We never had children, had no family around, and I needed a change. Thirty years later, and I still love this town. I just love the ocean, you know. I love being close to the water. I go to the beach a few times a week, you know. I read there, I knit there. It's quite nice. Oh! Your tea. Let me go get your tea. Hold on a moment, gentlemen."

She walked back into her kitchen and Corey looked at Robbie. "See? She's just a lonely old woman looking to talk."

"Yeah, I know," Robbie said. "We can appease her a few minutes more though."

"You're a softie sometimes, Denzel," Corey said with a laugh. "But yeah. A few minutes and then we're out."

They stayed and drank tea with the old woman, who they learned was named Hazel. Her late husband, James, wrote for the *San Antonio Express News* for twenty years. They never could have children, she told them. Sure, they had wanted to. But it wasn't in the cards, she said. And then, of course, "as my darn terrible luck would have it," she said, "James got heart disease and left this world without me." Her eyes were sad and lonely, Robbie thought while talking to her. She had a smile on her face as she spoke to him but Robbie sensed an emptiness behind it.

They said kind goodbyes to Hazel and went 10-8 from the call. Robbie's eyes were on Hazel's little brown house as the patrol car drove away. He opened up to Corey for the first time about his desire for a family.

"I don't want to be like that," Robbie said. "Old, alone. Sad. Didn't that woman seem sad? You, man, you have three kids, right?"

"I do. Jacob is ten, Mackenzie is eight, and Noah is five. Handful, man."

"Yeah," Robbie replied. "I'm sure. I want that too though."

"Oh yeah? You and Natasha trying?"

"We tried for years," Robbie answered. "We stopped trying though. It got too stressful. Natasha was so disappointed every month that went by. It was affecting her at work, affecting our relationship. It got to be too much. We've decided to adopt now. We were just placed on a waitlist for a kid."

"I had no idea, Jackson," Corey said. "I think that's great though. Good luck to you, man. Any kid would be lucky to be adopted by you and Natasha."

Robbie had a hopeful smile on his face. He was excited. After years of being unsuccessful at getting pregnant, he knew this was their next step, and it felt right. It felt good to think about.

Radio traffic broke up his thoughts then. "Domestic, two streets from here," Corey said. "Let's roll."

A woman in her early twenties was sitting on her porch steps when they arrived. She wore a plain white T-shirt with what appeared to have fresh blood stains, holey jeans, and bare feet. Her eyes were swollen and her face was expressionless.

"I didn't call for no police," she said. As she spoke, Robbie noticed that her front teeth had been knocked out. Her gums appeared to be swollen, looked like they were freshly bleeding.

"Of course you didn't call, I called," a middle-aged woman called out, walking briskly over from the house next door, cigarette in hand.

"Officers, I heard my neighbor and her boyfriend fighting," she said. She took a drag of her Marlboro. "She'll never call you out here. But I will. Every time."

"Ma'am, I'm Officer Corey Hayes, with the Corpus Christi Police Department." He looked at Robbie. "This here is Officer Robbie Jackson. Can you tell me your name?"

"Melissa," she said, looking down at the porch steps. "But I go by Missy."

"All right, Missy," Corey said. "Would you want to tell us what happened here today?"

"Nothing happened here. I'm fine. No need for y'all to be here."

"Your front teeth were there last time I saw you," the neighbor said, flicking ashes on the dirt. "And looks like he jacked up your eyes real good too. Why do you let him treat you like a punching bag? Let these officers take that man away."

"I see blood on your shirt," Corey said. He raised his eyebrows at Robbie.

"I'll call for EMS," Robbie said, reaching for his radio.

"Yes, we will get you some medical attention," Corey said. "Thank you, Officer Jackson, for getting on that. In the meantime, as he calls—Missy, where is the person who did this to you?"

"Don't call for medical attention—I'll refuse it. Stop. Seriously, I will refuse treatment. You are wasting your time."

Robbie put his radio down and looked at her. "Missy, they can be here in minutes. You aren't in any trouble. I think you need to be seen."

"No I don't," she said. "Officers, there is nothing wrong here. My neighbor is crazy. Get on your way, I'm sure you have other things to do."

Robbie and Corey looked at each other. Then Robbie gave his attention back to the neighbor. "You say the boyfriend did this? Did you witness it? Is he inside?"

"There is no one inside, he left," Missy said, still looking down at the porch steps. "And my crazy neighbor saw nothing."

"I didn't see the beating, Officers, but the yelling was so loud coming from their house, I know it was him. And why else would he run off? He's scared of y'all, that's why."

"She's crazy, Officers," Missy said again. "And look, my man isn't here. See the driveway? Empty. He's gone. Maybe gone forever, thanks to her, sticking her nose where it doesn't belong."

The neighbor shook her head and then let her cigarette butt fall to the ground, putting it out with her fuzzy house shoe. "Yeah, I did see him drive away," she said. "He sped off like a bat out of hell, just like he does after every big fight. Low-life coward. He knows I'll call you because I always do. He's gonna kill her one of these days. Enough is never enough for her. But I'll keep calling. Maybe one of these days she'll wake up and realize she needs to press charges. I'll keep calling." With that, she turned around and walked back to her house.

Corey sighed. He knew this scene too well. He knew he couldn't go try and find a man whom this beaten girl refused to press charges against. He knew he needed probable cause, and although he could speculate and assume the neighbor knew what she heard, he knew she didn't see it. And they could do nothing to help her.

"If you need us, you know how to get us here," Robbie said to the woman. "We want to help you."

"Take care of yourself, Missy," Corey said.

She didn't look up at them as they spoke. She continued a vacant stare, a look of nothing. Robbie couldn't help but wonder what she was thinking.

"I'll never understand, man," he said to Corey when they were back in the patrol car.

"Me neither, Denzel," Corey said, looking down as he worked on the report. "Me neither."

Corey put down the pen he had started writing the report with and looked at Robbie. "I have an aunt like that though. She stayed with a man who beat the crap out of her. Her boyfriend would beat her up every single time he drank too much—which was all the time, mind you—and she would never leave. Drove my whole family crazy. We tried to get her help, tried to get her to leave. Tried to get her to press charges when she ended up in the hospital this one time because of him. She always refused and always went back to him. So damn stupid. Guy ended up dead after drunk driving his truck into a tree. None of us went to the funeral, we were happy to have him gone forever. Good riddance, asshole. You know? But my aunt got so mad at us for skipping out on the funeral, she still doesn't speak to us. She said he was the love of her life and we should have gone to pay our respects to him."

Robbie shook his head. "Makes no damn sense," he said.

"Nope. Sure doesn't. I'm never going to understand it, so I don't even try."

"That girl looks like she used to be pretty, too, before she became a punching bag," Robbie said. "She probably could have any guy. Wonder why she sticks with the one that beats the crap out of her. Makes no sense."

"Brother, does anything we see make sense?" Corey started writing again.

Robbie laughed. "No. No, I guess it doesn't."

CHAPTER 7

"LET'S GO HAVE SEVEN TOGETHER," Rodriguez said. He was speaking to Jacobs, who was especially quiet at show-up that afternoon and his curiosity got the best of him.

Mandy and Adrian graduated the police academy together. Because of that, and because they were some of the few non-married, kid-less cops on the shift, they got along well and rode out together often.

"Who else is going?" she asked.

"Why—your boyfriend doesn't want for you to eat one-on-one with me anymore? He's jealous?" he joked.

It was known among the shift that Mandy's boyfriend, with whom she was in a long-distance relationship—was often giving Mandy grief over the fact that she worked primarily with men. She often complained about his lack of trust.

"Just asking," she said back at him, annoyed. "You know, half the time you all joke he isn't even real, the other half you're giving me crap about him being a jealous guy. It's old now, Rod."

"What, you can complain about him, but I can't joke about him?" Adrian said. "Fine. I'll stop giving you a hard time. And yes, you'd be eating with JUST ME. But don't worry. I won't spit any game at you . . . this time."

She rolled her eyes at him.

"Jacobs, you know I'm messing with you, come on," he said. "I'll stop. For real this time. I'll stop joking. Let's go eat."

"You don't know when to quit," she said. "But fine. I'll go seven with you, but only because I'm seriously starving. Where do you want to eat?"

"Fridays."

"Fridays? Why Fridays? We never eat there."

"I do now that I met a hot waitress who works there, who I know is working there right now, who I may or may not wish to see . . ."

"Of course," she said. "Of course it would be a girl. Why am I not surprised? Sure. Fridays it is, Rod."

They sat in a booth and Mandy could tell right away which waitress had given Adrian a reason to go there. Her makeup was caked on and included hot pink lip gloss with glitter in it, her hair was bleached an unnatural shade of blonde, and her breasts were pushed up so high it looked uncomfortable. She had long fake nails painted a neon glittery pink. They matched her lips. Mandy wondered how she managed to do anything with nails that long. Typical "flavor of the week" girl for Rodriguez.

She walked right over to the booth. "Officer Rodriguez, oh my, I can't believe you're here!"

"I told you, beautiful, call me Adrian," he said.

She giggled. "Okay, Adrian." She looked at Mandy. "Oh hi, I'm Chantel," she said.

Mandy wouldn't look her directly in the eyes. Or smile. In a monotone voice, she replied to Chantel with "Officer Jacobs. I work with Officer Rodriguez."

"Nice to meet you, Officer Jacobs. Can I get you both something to drink?"

After taking drink orders and walking off, Adrian told Mandy to lighten up.

"Be nice to Chantel," he said.

She rolled her eyes.

"I can tell you're having a bad day, Jacobs. But it ain't her fault. Come on. I like her."

"Oh, please. You like her now. Next week you'll avoid this place like the plague because you will have moved on to the next tramp."

"Whoa, whoa. Harsh, Jacobs," he said. "Harsh."

He shook his head and pressed his lips together.

"Tell me what's bothering you, Jacobs," he said then. "Spit it out."

Mandy sighed. She looked up from her menu at him.

"I'm sorry. I shouldn't have said that. You're right, it was harsh. And she doesn't deserve my bad attitude."

"So are you gonna tell me what's wrong, or what?"

Chantel brought the drinks over then.

"Officer Jacobs, your tea," she said. She then put Adrian's Dr Pepper in front of him, letting her hand linger after placing it on the table. Adrian took note, grabbed her hand, and kissed it. Chantel giggled.

Mandy wanted to roll her eyes then, but instead looked at Chantel and forced a smile. "You can call me Mandy," she said. "And thank you, Chantel."

Chantel's face lit up, as if the kindness of Mandy in that moment was the best thing that had ever happened to her. "Well, Adrian and Mandy—are you two ready to order?"

After walking away a second time to enter their food orders, Mandy started to open up.

"Ryan and I aren't doing so great," she said.

"Ah. So that explains it. I could tell something was wrong with you. Sorry to hear, Jacobs."

"Yeah. I mean, long distance is hard. That's no secret. I knew it would be hard. But it's also this job. He doesn't get it. Like, I try to talk to him about what I do, and he only cares about the fact that I work around dudes all day. I can't talk to him about work without a fight. It's hard. I want to talk to him, really. Like share my days with him, you know? But he doesn't hear me when I talk. Ugh. That make sense at all?"

"Yeah, it makes sense. I feel ya. Man, Jacobs, I really wish I had advice, but I don't do the relationship thing well, you know? But I hope it gets better for you. I really do."

"Thanks, Rod. And I *know* you don't do the relationship thing well. About that. This Chantel girl, she actually seems to be nice. I think I misjudged her when I came in here today. You be nice to her. Okay?"

Adrian laughed. "Yeah, okay."

"I'm serious, Rod. Don't screw her over. Got it?"

"Okay, okay. Geez, Jacobs. You sound like my mama."

"Whatever, Rodriguez," she said, smiling.

Chantel arrived back at the table with their plates.

"So, beautiful, you gonna let me take you to dinner soon, or what?" Adrian asked her after she set the plates down.

Chantel blushed and smiled. "Oh, Adrian, I'd love to go to dinner with you," she answered.

"Great," he said back. "How's this Saturday night?"

"That's perfect," she answered.

"Perfect indeed, beautiful," he said with a wink. "It's a date."

Don't roll your eyes, don't roll your eyes, don't roll your eyes . . . Mandy thought to herself. *That is just how Rodriguez talks, and some women like it.*

Mandy gave her best smile to Chantel then. "Thank you, Chantel. May I bug you for a refill of tea?"

Chantel came out of the trance she was in, looking at Adrian. "Oh, yes, of course!" she said, and she happily took Mandy's glass to go refill it. "Be right back."

***

AS SOON AS LUNCH WAS FINISHED, radio traffic let them know that White was in a vehicle pursuit.

"Let's roll to back him up," Mandy said to Adrian. They lit up their patrol lights and blew that way. Adrian had a moment of regret for the amount of French fries he'd devoured as Mandy made a quick sharp turn down a narrow road. He shook off the thought of his rumbling stomach and paid attention to where they were heading.

It was no secret that Brian White was the unliked man on the shift. He wasn't typically invited to the smaller get-togethers and birthday parties that the Bravo 400s had. When he was invited, he would either come late and leave early, or skip out altogether. His reputation was one of an arrogant jerk. But in that moment—when his shift-mates were rushing to back him up for a chase—that reputation washed away. He was their brother. No matter what. Jacobs and Rodriguez had tunnel vision in the patrol car in that moment to get to him. And they did just that, three minutes after they heard the call that he was in a pursuit. They had heard Brian call out that the suspect had wrecked out and started running away on foot. Brian could be heard panting on the radio, telling his location of where he was now on a foot pursuit. Mandy and Adrian saw his patrol car was on the side of the road, door swung open, as they rolled up to where he was. He was cuffing an overweight man on the ground when they spotted him.

"He's got him," Mandy said to Adrian. As they walked that way, White shouted, "He was dropping dope out of his pockets while I was chasing him," and immediately Rodriguez started looking around with his flashlight. He found three plastic baggies rather quickly, as they weren't far from where the man had been cuffed, and picked them up. "Looks like marijuana here, and cocaine in this one," Rodriguez said.

After the suspect was in the vehicle, Mandy asked Brian, "You good, White?"

"Yeah, Jacobs, I am," he answered. "That fat slob was easy to chase. I'm a marine, remember? He had nothing on me." He shook his head and gave a short chuckle. "That piece of shit didn't have nothing on me. He made it too easy. I could outrun both of you two, you know. Try me. We'll race one of these days, you'll see. I can smoke anybody."

"Ah, there's that pride we all love to hear from you, White," she said.

"Damn straight, Jacobs," Brian said.

Adrian smiled and shook his head. "Bro, I don't think she means the good pride," he said, laughing.

"Is there a bad pride, Rodriguez?" White asked.

Mandy put her hand on Brian's shoulder. "Brother, look up the definition of humility," she said. "And hey, I'm really glad you're good. Let's roll, Rod."

"He isn't as bad as people say he is," Adrian said to Mandy after they returned to their patrol car.

"Oh, he isn't?" Mandy asked, eyebrows raised. "You've got a thing for White now?"

"Ha, ha. Real funny, Jacobs," he said. "Nah. I just mean that I don't think he's that bad. I know he acts all cocky and stuff sometimes, but he can be all right too."

"Rod, he was a marine supply guy that never saw combat but talks as if he's some kind of war hero. And he's divorced because he left his wife for gaining too much weight. You know that, right?"

"Jacobs, you believe that garbage? You think that's true, huh?"

"Well, why wouldn't it be? His character isn't exactly stellar, Rod. What—he told you something different?"

"Yeah. You know what? We hung out once."

"Whaaat? When? White doesn't hang out with anyone. You have some secret meet-up or something?"

"Nah. I was out with an old college buddy actually. At Mulligan's. He ditched me after his girl called him, all mad that he was out without her. See why I don't want to be tied down? Nonsense like that. Anyway, he bailed on me, and there were no hotties there, so I was gonna call it a night. But then I notice White sitting at a table alone. I was gonna walk by him, act like I didn't see him, you know—but he saw me, made eye contact. So I felt obligated. I sat down with him."

Mandy raised her eyebrows. "And how did that go?"

"He bought me a beer. Told me he was there because it would've been his two-year wedding anniversary, had he not gotten divorced."

"Oh boo-freakin'—hoo," Mandy said. "Shouldn't have left his wife just because she gained weight. Sorry, not sorry."

"Well, that's just it," Adrian said. "He told me a different story. He does say that his wife got too fat—I know. But he told me that night that she was actually the one that left him. He just doesn't tell people the real version of what happened because he's too embarrassed."

"You're kidding," Mandy said.

"No, I'm telling you what he told me," he said. "She left him. Okay, so here is the part you have to swear you won't repeat."

Mandy lowered her eyebrows in confusion. "Okay . . ."

"She left him for a woman."

"Are you messing with me, or are you for real right now?" Mandy asked. "Seriously, Rod, I don't have time for your stupid jokes right now."

"I'm one hundred percent for real."

It took Mandy a moment to respond. ". . . Whoa. Holy crap. I had no idea. I guess I see how that could be embarrassing. Wow."

"I know. He'd rather people believe he left her because she got fat than the truth—she left him for a woman. He married a lesbian and didn't even know it."

"Well, damn, Rod," Mandy said. "Now I sort of feel bad for the guy. Sort of. He could choose to be less arrogant though, you know? He acts like such a cocky jerk. He could be better. Maybe even meet someone again—someone who likes dudes."

She smirked and Adrian laughed.

"Yeah," he said. "Just his way of dealing with it though. Everyone has their ways, Jacobs."

"Yeah, I guess so . . ." Mandy replied.

CHAPTER 8

"GOOD MORNING, HONEY, today marks the official start of the safe zone," Leah said to Brandon when he woke up one late morning after a work night. "We can share our baby news!"

"Second trimester already," Brandon replied. "Did that go by fast for you too?"

"Not really, I've been sick as a dog," Leah said. "But so glad time is flying for you. Nice."

Brandon hugged her. "I'm sorry, babe, that you've been so sick. Really, I am. But I'm glad first trimester is over and done with. Hopefully you'll get some relief from all the nausea."

"Yeah. It is starting to ease. I just had to give you a little grief." She smiled at him and he smiled back.

"So, who are we calling first?"

"No one yet," Leah answered. "I want to start by telling Cassie, and she and I are hanging out later—remember? Moms' night away? So I'll get to tell her in person."

"Yeah—I remember," Brandon said. "Where you two going again?"

"New Mexican place across from Barnes and Noble," she said. "We'll eat, then go browse books after, then we'll be home."

"Sounds good," Brandon said. "Since you ladies are ditching us husbands and kids, I'll see if Corey wants to bring his rugrats over for some pizza."

"That'll be fun for you all," she said. "But remember it isn't the weekend for everyone, their kids are school age. Try not to keep them up all night."

"We wouldn't, Leah," he said. "You think Corey and I can't get our kids to bed at a reasonable hour unless you moms are here to dictate bedtime?"

"Well," she said, "you have been known to completely disregard bedtime."

"I have no idea what you're talking about." Brandon smiled. "But okay, ma'am. Strict bedtimes to be enforced by the dads tonight. You've got it."

"Thank you, handsome husband," Leah said.

Brandon kissed her. "You're welcome, beautiful wife."

***

"LEAH, I'M SO GLAD TO GET away from the house with you today," Cassie said after she'd dropped her husband and three kids with Leah's husband and they had driven off for their evening out.

"Oh, me too," Leah said. "I needed a break. I was about to lose my mind if I didn't have some kid-free time. Know what I mean?"

"Oh, I know what you mean," Cassie said. "Same here. And also . . . I'm sorry about the last time we were together."

Leah had a confused expression. "Sorry for what?"

"Christmas party night—I drank too much and was acting like an idiot. I'm so embarrassed. My behavior was terrible."

"Oh, please, Cassie. No need to apologize. You were tipsy, yes, but you didn't have bad behavior. You've seen me worse, I'm sure."

"No, no, I haven't," Cassie said. "You're a lightweight like me but you manage to at least still walk properly after you've had a few. Me, I nearly busted my face on your porch after. Thank the Lord for my husband and his crazy reflexes or I might not have teeth right now." She laughed.

Leah laughed too. "Ah, that was a fun night. Cassie—I probably would have been tipsy right along with you. Our kids were gone for the night. But—I wasn't really drinking any of the wine you were giving me. I was faking it."

Now Cassie had the confused expression on her face. "Faking it?"

"Yes," Leah said. "I have news."

Cassie's face lit up then. "Oh my goodness, Leah—are you about to tell me what I think you're about to tell me?"

"Well, what do you think I'm about to tell you?"

"That you and Brandon are catching up to me and Corey and made baby number three?"

Leah smiled. "You've guessed it," she said.

"Ahhh!" Cassie had a huge grin on her face. "How exciting! Congratulations, my friend! When are you due?"

"Late July," Leah said. "It'll be hot as heck outside. I wasn't thinking this whole 'summer baby' thing through. I'm going to be a sweaty, miserable whale at the end! But . . . we're excited. And I'm happy to be getting our news out there now. I hated keeping it from you especially, but you know that I had that miscarriage before, and it just scared me off from sharing pregnancy news too quickly."

"Of course," Cassie said. "I understand. Late July, how fun. Oh, I'll bet it's a boy. Yep. I'm calling it now. Is Brandon super excited?"

"Yeah, he is," she answered. "And we just told the girls last week, they're really excited too."

"Ahh, I can't believe it," Cassie said. "Seeing you prego is totally going to give me baby fever, Leah. Ha."

"Well, maybe you aren't done," Leah said. "You think Corey would go for a fourth baby?"

"Ha! You know, actually, he would," Cassie said. "He totally wanted to keep having kids. And he's an amazing dad, you know. But I had terrible pregnancies and wanted to call it quits after Noah, so we did. But . . . he's five now, so it's been a while. I don't know. I guess you never know. But hey—enough about me. Let's talk more about you! Miss Prego. How have you been feeling lately?"

"A little better now than I was," Leah said. "I was really sick at first. But it's slowly been getting easier."

"Oh good, I'm glad to hear that. And glad to hear you have baby number three coming. I'm so happy for you, Leah."

"Thank you, Cassie. So tell me. What's new with you?"

"Same old, mostly. You know. Kids are back to school after two weeks of Christmas break, and they still give me a hard time every morning because they want to sleep in. But all is well. I can't complain. Corey and I are doing really well, too. We had been fighting a lot, you remember—but it was just us taking the stress of kids out on each other, I think. I tend to get overwhelmed with our kids and forget that he isn't exactly on vacation when he's out of the house—he has a rough job too."

Leah nodded. "I can be the same way. I feel you. I take stress out on Brandon. It's easy to forget sometimes what they do. Like you said, it's easy to get caught up in the difficulties of being home with the kids and totally forget that they're getting called pigs, and dealing with drunk people . . . and everything else. You know."

"Yeah, I do know. It's really nice to be able to talk about it. That's why we should do this more often—it's nice to have a friend that's a mom and cop's wife too."

"Agreed," Leah said.

Cassie laughed. "Ah, I was trying to talk to another PTO mom recently—sharing a story about the stomach flu. We were both complaining about kid vomit everywhere—and I was like, 'yeah, but my husband had a drunk transient throw up in the back of his patrol car, so I guess we don't have it that bad, eh?'" She laughed again. "I wish you could have seen the way she looked at me. She was half confused, half disgusted, full on thinking I'm a weirdo. I told myself after that—I need to save certain stories for fellow cop spouses."

Leah was laughing too. "Oh, I'll bet you grossed her out," she said. "That's too funny. Yeah, people who aren't married to cops don't get it."

"No, they don't quite get it," Cassie said. Her smile changed then. She looked down and bit the inside of her cheek.

"What is it, Cassie?" Leah asked. "You look upset all of a sudden."

"Oh, it's nothing," Cassie answered. "It's just—I thought of another incident recently—at a garage sale, of all places. I went last Saturday to browse. You know I like finding fun old stuff. Anyway, I overheard a couple talking about the shooting in Dallas—you know, the teenager who pointed his BB gun at police and was killed?"

"I know that story, yes," Leah answered. "Awful. But the police didn't know it was a BB gun. They look so real these days."

"I know," Cassie said. "I know you know too. But this couple—they called the cop a murderer. I overheard them call him a murderer. I wanted to scream at them. Like, what was the cop supposed to do, be shot first to find out it was a BB gun and not something else? I swear, that's what people want. They don't want our husbands to defend themselves."

Leah nodded in agreement. "I know, Cassie. It's frustrating. But people are just really ignorant. They have no idea what it's like. Cops have to make split-second decisions that could save or end their lives. And no one gets it unless they do it. So did you say anything? To the people at the garage sale?"

"I came close. I looked over at them, and they noticed me staring. I opened my mouth to talk, and then said nothing. I just walked away and got in my car."

"Probably for the best," Leah said.

"Of course," Cassie said. "One of these days the anti-cop talk is going to make me snap, though."

"I hear that," Leah responded.

***

BACK AT LEAH AND BRANDON'S house, the Hayes kids and the Morgan kids were happily eating cheese pizza and drinking apple juice boxes as the dads enjoyed their meat lover's pizza and Shiner Bock.

"So," Brandon said, "since the wife said I can let the cat out of the bag—I'll tell you first—I knocked Leah up again. Baby number three is on the way."

"Hey, congrats, buddy," Corey said with a mouth full of pizza. "That's awesome."

"Thanks, dude," Brandon said, sipping his beer. "I'm hoping I get a boy this time."

Corey nodded. "Yeah—I'll bet you do. Boys are fun but they're also kind of crazy."

Brandon laughed. He looked over at the kids, all stuffing their faces with pizza. They were out of earshot from their dads.

"All kids are a little crazy though, right? But in a good way."

"Yeah, if there is such a thing as 'a little crazy in a good way,' bro."

Both men just smiled, and continued to munch on pizza and drink their beer. Despite the fact that they were both on daddy duty, it was a relaxing evening. Both men appreciated how easy their friendship was.

CHAPTER 9

"AWW, ROOK, AREN'T YOU LUCKY to have Valentine's Day fall on our day off this year," Joe said to Danny on the eve of the shift's weekend.

"Dude—Zavala—you have no right to make fun of me, you know you're more of a girl than me when it comes to stuff like this."

Chris, Corey, and Brandon all started laughing. It was almost show-up time and they were still burning minutes goofing off before Sarge and Corporal arrived.

"Yeah, Zavala, Perales is right," Chris said. "What mushy date you got planned for Gloria this year, huh? Candlelit bubble bath with Kenny G on the stereo?"

The guys laughed some more.

"Hey, hey, don't hate just because my Gloria and I have a romantic life to be envied," Joe said. "Besides, this is a conversation between Perales and me."

Joe looked at Danny. "So, for real. What you got planned, bro?"

Chris interrupted them. "Whoa there, Joe, we have romantic lives too, just not Hallmark phony holiday garbage. Trust me, my wife doesn't like that corny crap either. Okay, Perales. Continue, please. What's up with you and the girlfriend?"

"You guys are all too much sometimes," Danny said, shaking his head. "All right, nosy asses. If you must know, I am taking Sierra out for Valentine's Day, to a nice dinner. And it's getting real, y'all. Make fun of me if you want. But Sierra, she's the one. I'm serious."

"Awwww, rook," Joe said, grabbing Danny's shoulder. "Good for you, bud. You're still young and good-looking and could play the field like Rod does, but you don't. One-woman man. I get it, man, I'm the same way. I know I give you a lot of grief but I'm happy for you, man."

"Yeah—try not to screw it up," Brian said from the back of the room.

Joe turned his head toward Brian. "Eavesdropping, White?"

"Come sit by us if you wanna talk, White," Danny said.

"I'm good back here," Brian replied.

The rest of the shift started to trickle in then.

"All right, quiet everyone," Sarge said, walking in, Corporal right behind him. "Corporal Harris has BOLOs for you. Harris?"

"Yes, Sarge. Two BOLOs," Jared said, while the pictures of the fliers came up on the projector screen. "One on the left, suspect is a white male, bald, date of birth September 5, 1967, that one is wanted for vehicle theft. Dirtbag on the right is wanted for sexual abuse of a minor. Description is Hispanic male, short guy—only five foot three inches tall, date of birth June 18, 1984."

"All right," Sarge said. "I have nothing else for you at this time. Let's get to work, and try to be off on time. All right? All right."

The shift trickled out. After the last man was out, Jared starting talking to Gabe. He didn't realize Joe was outside of the room still, texting on his cell phone. Joe was returning a text to his wife but overheard his Corporal and Sarge talking, and couldn't help but listen in.

"Happy about the move, or what?" he heard Jared say.

"Eh, it's going to be different," Gabe answered. "No one is going to like me anymore. Not that I care. But you know it's true."

"Internal Affairs guys get a bad rep, I know," Jared said. "But we know you. We'll still always have your back. It's going to suck to work for someone else now. I've gotten used to you."

"Oh, you'll get used to someone else real quick," Gabe said.

"Yeah. So when are you telling the shift?"

"Soon," Gabe said. "But not today. Soon."

"I don't think they'll receive the news with too much enthusiasm, Sarge, just sayin'."

"Oh, they'll be just fine," Gabe replied. "Besides, they'll still have you. Coolest corporal in the department, right? Isn't that your official title?"

Jared shook his head and laughed. "I don't know about that."

Joe knew he needed to hurry out then, before they realized he had been outside the door and listening to everything. *Dang, Sarge is leaving us for Internal Affairs?* he thought to himself. *That sucks.*

***

ROBBIE JACKSON RODE with Chris Janacek that evening. Shortly after the daylight faded a call came up on the computer screen that was two streets away from where they were patrolling.

"Gotta take this one, we're close by," Chris said, looking at the computer screen in the patrol car.

"Some guy is going door to door scaring people? Sun barely just went down and the crazies are already out. Okay. Let's roll," Robbie said.

As soon as they pulled onto the street of the call, they could see a group of people standing in front of one of the homes. Five people total, all waving their arms in the air frantically to get Chris and Robbie over to them. Three men and two women. Chris parked the patrol car along the curb opposite of the crowd and both men hopped out.

"Officers, Officers, this drunken homeless man was kicking on all of our doors," one of the women said. "Scaring all of us and all the neighborhood kids to death. He's loud, too. Screaming and yelling like he's crazy or something."

"Can you tell us where he is now?" Chris asked, looking around.

The group of people didn't need to answer, because as soon as Chris finished asking, they spotted him. He was a good distance from them all, almost on the opposite end of the street. Both Robbie and Chris walked quickly over to him. He was holding a tallboy in a paper sack. He reeked of alcohol and body odor. He was older, and a great big burly man. Looked to be at least 350 pounds. He had long white dirty hair and a white beard.

"Dude, Santa Claus himself is terrorizing the street," Chris joked under his breath as they got closer.

Robbie was the first to speak to him. "You're under arrest," Robbie said, cuffs in hand.

The man then turned and looked at both of them. He paused for a moment. Then he threw his can at them as hard as his drunken self could muster. His aim was terrible, the can barely scraping by Robbie's left boot. The man then started running the opposite direction, screaming and flailing his arms.

He was loud, very loud. But he wasn't very fast. It didn't take any time for Robbie and Chris to catch up to him. "Stop! You're under arrest!" Robbie yelled out.

The man wasn't giving up. Though Robbie had initially gotten a hold of his arm, he started trying to wiggle out of his hold. Then he started kicking at both officers. "He's freakishly strong for a big old man," Robbie said. Chris managed to grab his radio with his free hand. "Suspect is fighting us," he said. Brian White had been close to the location of the call as well, so it took him no time to arrive for backup.

"Stop resisting!" Chris yelled out. They were in the middle of the street trying to wrangle a 350-pound drunken man. It was tiring. The man's strength continued to surprise them. He was violently kicking now as they tried to put cuffs on him. They slammed him on the ground.

Brian rolled up behind them, leaving his lights on as he parked, and quickly got out of his patrol car to assist with the call. He heard a car approaching from behind him and turned around. An old black Nissan Xterra was coming up and the driver didn't see either Brian's lights or the men wrestling in the middle of the street. Brian saw the driver, a young guy, wasn't looking up at all, but was glued to his cell phone. The car was headed straight for Robbie, Chris, and the man they were struggling to arrest.

"SLOW DOWN!" Brian yelled out, running next to the car, flailing his arms like a crazy person, trying to get the driver's attention. Finally the kid looked up from his phone and swerved just enough, causing his car to pop up on the curb on the left side of the old residential street. He didn't stop. Just straightened out his car and kept driving.

Just as Robbie had finally pinned Santa's arms down successfully and cuffed him he felt a quick strong gush of wind to the left of his face and felt as though he had been scraped. Chris was still behind him to the right, holding the old man's lower half down. Robbie looked up. He saw the Xterra drive away and realized it had missed him by inches. His heart jumped and he took a quick deep breath. "Whoa," he whispered.

"We need to get him out of the damn road," he heard Brian White yell from behind as he ran up to them. "Next car that drives by is going to take us all out."

The three of them maneuvered the drunken Santa into the back of the patrol car.

"Jackson, dude, did you know you missed your head being taken off by a car by *inches*?" Brian asked as he belted the cuffed man into the back of the patrol car. "I was waving my arms around like a bat-shit crazy person and got him to swerve just enough not to hit you. He was looking at his freakin' phone, man. Not paying attention. He almost killed you."

Robbie nodded. "Yeah. I swear, I felt something scrape my cheek," he said, putting his hand up to where his face met his ear. "It took me a minute to realize it was a car. Thanks, White. For being here. For getting him to swerve."

"Yeah, no problem, Jackson," Brian replied.

"You all right, man?" Chris asked as they got back into the patrol car to drive the big drunk guy to jail.

"Fine. Yeah. Hell, Janacek. That might've been my closest call yet."

"I know," Chris said. "That was crazy. I didn't see the car until it was already in front of us. White wasn't lying, it came close to taking your head off, Denzel."

"Yeah. Couple of inches closer to me and I'd be a dead man. But I was spared for today. I'll call it a win, Janacek." He made a fist and gave Chris a hand-pound.

Chris grinned at him. "For sure, man, a win."

Robbie shook his head. He looked down and twisted his wedding ring around for a minute. "My wife and I are starting the adoption process, man. Starting my family. Not trying to die today on the street."

"Nope, not today," Chris said. "Not today."

It was quiet as both men quietly regrouped. Chris was the first to start talking again. "Hey. Good on you, man, choosing to adopt. I think that's awesome."

Robbie nodded. "I only wish we would've started this whole process sooner. We spent years trying to get pregnant. Years. Wore us down. Especially Natasha, it really wore her down. She's longed to be a mother for as long as I've known her. But now, now we're on the track to become parents. And it feels right. You know? Just feels right."

"Man, you never told me that you and Natasha tried for so long," Chris said. "I honestly assumed you were kid-free by choice. I'm sorry, man. But I'm glad for you, doing the adoption thing. Jackson, you and your wife are going to make great parents. For real."

"Thanks, man. We've been hearing that a lot lately. And you know something? I believe it."

Chris pulled the patrol car into the jail parking lot. "All righty, Denzel," he said. "Let's get Santa Claus booked."

Robbie laughed. "Yeah, let's do that."

CHAPTER 10

DANNY HAD CHOSEN TO TAKE Sierra to the Water Street Seafood Company for Valentine's Day. She had mentioned on their first date that it was her favorite restaurant.

"Let's get oysters on the half shell," she said to him as they slid into their booth. "And martinis. Want to? Doesn't that sound good?"

Danny smiled at Sierra. She was wearing a pale pink short-sleeved dress that was loose and had pockets. She wore a long gold necklace and matching gold earrings. Her long, caramel-colored hair was curled lightly and it seemed to just float on her shoulders and back. She wore clear lip gloss and a tiny bit of pink shimmer on her eyes, highlighting the golden brown hue. She was beautiful. He couldn't believe how lucky he was.

"Sounds really good," he answered.

"Good. We'll get the oysters to start, and . . . oh, Danny. You have to try the mahi-mahi. It's so good. Want to try it?"

"I do want to try it," he said. "Sounds great."

She folded her menu and set it down. Then she reached her hands across the table to hold his.

"This is nice, Danny. Being here with you. On Valentine's Day. You're my favorite Valentine so far." She giggled.

"So far, huh? Well, same to you, Sierra. You're my favorite so far too."

Her smile then started to fade and she looked down.

"Hey, what's wrong?" Danny asked.

She pulled her hands from his and set them in her lap.

"Nothing, really. I mean, I guess I'm just a little afraid of how quickly I've fallen for you."

"Sierra, I'm on the same page. I feel strongly for you too."

"Yeah, I think I know," she said. "But I've been worried, you know, that this can't actually work. Not for long anyway."

"Why? Why can't it work?"

She started biting the inside of her cheek. Then she sighed.

"Well, because of my family. My mom."

Danny's eyebrows lowered in confusion. "What? Sierra, I've met your parents and like them both. What are you talking about? Does she not like me? She gave me the impression that she did."

"Oh, she likes you, she does."

"Then what are you talking about?"

"Danny, I'm sorry I didn't tell you before. But my mom, she has a criminal record. She's been to prison."

"Okay . . ." Danny said, waiting for more. He was visibly confused. He looked at Sierra in anticipation of more to the story, but she just sat there quietly.

"What else?" Danny asked.

"Doesn't that make you want to run?" Sierra asked.

"Why would that make me want to run?"

"Because you're a cop," Sierra answered. "I figured a cop wouldn't want to date a convicted felon's daughter."

Danny shook his head and then smiled. He reached across the table and signaled for Sierra to give him her hands again. She obliged.

"I'm not going anywhere, especially not because your mom made a mistake a long time ago," he said. "And I'm dating you—not your mom."

Sierra started to smile and looked relieved.

"I can't believe you actually thought that would change my feelings for you," Danny said. "And by the way—I seriously can't believe your mom has been to prison. You said she's a felon? I can't see her as anything but the sweet lady who makes the best chicken enchiladas I've ever had. You mind telling me why she went to prison?"

"She sold drugs. I don't know what kind, or how much, or any of those details. All I know is it was bad enough for two years in prison. It was before I was born. I didn't even know this about her until I was eighteen."

"Wow," Danny said. "I would have never, ever guessed that about your mom."

"I know. It shocked me. She kept it a secret for a long time. It was actually because of the last election that I even found out. I was eighteen, and excited to be able to vote for the first time. I know, I'm a dork. Don't make fun of me for that. But I was super excited to vote, and wanted her to go with me. She kept telling me no, that she didn't want to vote. And I pressed her, and pressed her, for days, weeks, maybe. Then she finally told me that she wouldn't go vote because she *couldn't* go vote, because she's a convicted felon and lost that right. I was completely shocked. And then sad for her, because she couldn't vote. Silly, right? I'm rambling now, aren't I. Sorry, Danny. But now you know. You're dating the daughter of a convicted felon."

"Sierra," Danny said, "I'm dating the daughter of a wonderful woman who made some mistakes many years ago."

"Wow, Danny. In my mind I imagined this conversation going another way. I was embarrassed to tell you, but wanted to get it out there before our relationship went any further. I didn't expect for you to hear my family drama and react so well. Thank you for being so awesome. I'm relieved. And so happy."

"I'm glad you're happy," Danny said. "But I'm not that awesome. I have family drama of my own, you know."

"Oh yeah? You've got criminals for parental units too?"

"Ha—not that I know of," he said. "But, if I'm being truthful, I'm closer to my dog, Lexi, than to my parents. And I have no siblings, you know that."

"To be fair, Lexi is the coolest dog I've ever met," Sierra said. "But in all seriousness—why is it that you aren't close to your parents?"

"My parents never wanted kids, they let that be known all the time," he said. "I was always referred to as 'the mistake.' Then one day my dad up and left. Ran off with his secretary and started a new life. I haven't seen him since then, actually . . . Anyway, my mom blamed me. She actually told me once that if she would've just been smart enough to abort me, her marriage would have been kept intact."

"Oh, Danny. I'm so sorry," Sierra said.

He had a sadness in his eyes she hadn't seen before. She stood up and moved to his side of the booth. She took his face in her hands and kissed him.

"You know something?" she asked. "I love you, Danny Perales."

He was taken aback a bit. He smiled.

"I love you too, Sierra Medina," he said. "I was going to be the one to say it first. You beat me to it."

They embraced. After the server brought the mahi-mahi entrees to the table, Sierra returned to her side of the booth.

"This is my favorite date so far," Sierra said.

"Mine too," Danny said back. "So far."

***

VALENTINE'S DAY AT THE HAYES residence was mostly just an ordinary day. Corey did, however, surprise Cassie with a dozen red roses. He'd picked them up from the grocery store, found an old vase, and made the arrangement himself. He was quite proud when she walked in and saw them.

"Wow, Corey, you haven't brought me flowers in forever," she said. She leaned over the vase and took in the smell of the roses. She loved roses, they were her favorite. So beautiful, so classic . . . "Wait . . . what did you do?"

"Ha, ha, very funny," Corey said to Cassie, pulling her in by her waist for a kiss. "I can't buy my wife roses on Valentine's Day unless I'm sorry for something?"

"I suppose you can," she replied, smiling up at him. "I'm just not used to it is all. We are usually on the same page about this holiday being a phony one. But I'll admit, they are beautiful. And you know roses are my favorite. Thank you, honey."

"You're welcome," Corey said back. "You deserve to get pretty flowers every once in a while, pretty girl."

"Now you're going to make me blush," Cassie said with a big grin. "All right. Now back to the business of what to feed our children for dinner. I know most restaurants are going to be busy tonight. Interested in just ordering some pizzas, staying in?"

"Did I hear you say pizza, Mom?" their youngest, Noah asked, walking into the kitchen holding a toy police car.

"Yes, buddy, you did," Cassie said.

"Yay! Pizza is my favorite! I'll tell Jacob and Mack!" He dropped his toy and went running back into the living room, where his sister and brother were busy watching Nickelodeon.

"Guys, we're ordering pizza!" he yelled.

"Pizza? Yum. Sounds good to me," Jacob said.

"Yeah, thanks, Mom and Dad!" Mackenzie yelled out.

"Noah, get back in here and get your police car, then I'll call Domino's," Cassie said. "You don't just throw your toys on the ground, bud."

He ran back into the kitchen and picked up the car. "Sorry, Mom. I won't do it again. This is my favorite toy, you wanna know why?"

"Why is it your favorite toy, Noah?" Corey asked his son.

"Because it's like what you drive, Dad!" Noah said. "And what Grandpa used to ride! And what I'm going to ride when I grow up!"

"Oh, you want to be a policeman now, Noah?" Corey asked his son. "Last week you wanted to be a pilot and fly big airplanes."

"I changed my mind," Noah said. "Your job seems cooler."

He patted his son's head. Cassie smiled at him as she dialed the number for pizza delivery.

"We have good kids, don't we," Corey said to his wife, matter-of-factly.

She nodded at him, as she held the phone up to her ear. "One large cheese, one large pepperoni, please. Yes, delivery. Forty-five minutes? Okay. Thank you." She gave their address and hung up the phone. "We do. You think that kid will be a third-generation police officer? Too early to tell, huh?"

Corey looked over at Noah. "If he wants to be a cop when he's grown, I'll support it," he said. "But if he doesn't that would be great too."

"Why do you say that? You love your job, don't you?"

"Most of the time, yes," he answered. "But it's not what you think it's going to be. I understand more about why my dad told me if I could see myself doing anything else, to do it. You go into law enforcement with this idea that you'll help people, and end up on calls all day that are actually doing very little to help people. Calls come in from people who are garbage, who are in bad situations because of their own actions."

Cassie nodded. "Well, I know what you do is hard, babe," she said. "But I am really proud of you. And proud of your dad. And if Noah wants to follow in yours and his footsteps, I'll be proud of him too. But the kid is five and can't keep his finger out of his nose, so we'll see what he amounts to." She smiled and kissed her husband on the cheek, then walked out to the living room.

"Kids," she said. "Dinner will be here soon. Turn the TV off, and clean up this mess of a living room. Your toys are everywhere. It looks like a daycare in here. Clean it up, then wash your hands, and then come into the kitchen."

"Aw, Mommy, we're watching *Paw Patrol*," Noah complained.

"Don't care," Cassie said. "TV off. Now."

"Okay, fine," he said then, getting up off the couch.

Mackenzie didn't say a word, just started picking up and taking toys to her room.

"These toys aren't mine, Mom," Jacob said.

"Don't care," Cassie said. "Help clean up anyway. Teamwork. Got it?"

Jacob rolled his eyes. "Fine."

"Roll your eyes again at me, son, and I'll take your tablet away for a month."

"Yes ma'am," Jacob said.

CHAPTER 11

ALEX MANG AND CHRIS JANACEK, always the early birds to work, were in show-up especially early the next work day and had time to kill. Alex had been playing a game on his smartphone but set it down when he noticed Chris walking in.

"Hey, Mang, how was your weekend?" Chris asked as he sat next to him.

"It was all right, Janacek. How was yours?"

"Fine, mostly," Chris said. "Would've been better if I hadn't been an idiot and let the kids overhear the damn news."

There had been an officer-involved shooting two days prior, in Houston. An unarmed black man was shot by an officer after a pursuit and fight. Details were still coming in about the entire series of events—but it didn't matter what had happened. All that was said by the media was: white officer, unarmed black man. Several riots had started that weekend in Houston. It was on every news channel. News cameras showed rioters looting stores, starting fires in the streets downtown, throwing rocks at police cars. It seemed to be all the news was talking about.

"Houston incident?" Alex asked.

"Yeah," Chris answered. "I don't know what I was thinking, having the news on. My oldest three saw the story, and it started a conversation that I hadn't exactly been ready for."

"I can't imagine," Alex said. "I have a hard time just with my mom, man. She called me upset over it all. She questions me all the time about this job but yesterday she laid it on thick on the phone. 'Why not med school, Alex?' she asked me. 'You could have been a surgeon, been better off financially than you are, and safer.' She nagged me for a good hour. But I have the luxury of ending the phone call and being done with hearing it. I'm sure it's harder with the kids, man. Sorry. Sounds rough."

Chris nodded. "They scare easily. They shouldn't have been watching the news . . . it's my fault. I forget sometimes that they are paying attention to the television too. The big ones—they know, of course, a little about what I do. But then the news comes on and shows mobs of people starting fires in the streets, throwing rocks at patrol cars, chanting 'F the police'—well, my kids don't know what to make of that."

"So, what did you tell them?"

"Not much, actually. Just not to worry. Kristin talked more to them. She prayed with them, then distracted all of them with a book. She's a champ at storytelling. She can do so many funny voices . . . she's good like that."

Alex smiled at Chris. "Maybe have Kristin call my mom and calm her down too."

"Ha—yeah. My wife. The worried-family-member whisperer."

Chris's face became somber then. "But Kristin gets worried sometimes too. Last night in bed, she told me that sometimes my job wears her down. Stresses her out. Scares her." He sighed. "So that was my time off. Kind of crappy."

The rest of the shift started to trickle in then.

"Talking about H-Town?" Brandon asked as he sat next to Chris.

"Yeah. Stresses the family out."

"I know, dude," Brandon said. "Leah begged me not to come in today. I left her crying. I thought briefly about calling in. But I'm here." He let out a big sigh.

"She'll be all right, Morgan," Chris said. "I'd text her more than usual tonight though. Check in, you know."

"Yeah, I know," he answered.

Sarge didn't stand at the podium this time, he just sat and watched as Corporal Harris addressed the shift.

"I'm sure you guys can guess that tension is high because of the media blowing up the story out of Houston," he said. "As always, head on a swivel. Watch your six. It's close enough to home that it will probably have an effect on us, unfortunately. You all know how this goes. Be safe, this should all fade away and it'll be business as usual soon. Sarge, anything to add?"

Sarge shook his head, looked down, and never opened his mouth.

"All right, get to work," Corporal said, and everyone left the room to head to their cars.

"He's quiet, I know," Mandy said to Adrian when they walked outside. "But usually not that quiet. It can't just be the Houston stuff going on keeping him quiet. What's up with him?"

"I heard he's leaving our shift," Joe chimed in, walking closely behind them. "Maybe that's got something to do with it."

"Leaving the shift? What? Who said that? Who's replacing him?" Adrian asked. Joe opened his mouth to answer him, but was interrupted by Mandy. "No, no—no gossiping to us, Zavala. Rumors are rumors. I'll believe it when I hear it from him. I hope that isn't true. I like our Sarge."

"Me too," Joe said. "We all do."

***

"PIGS! NOBODY CALLED YOU out here!" a man yelled out as Mandy and Adrian stepped out of their patrol car on a complaint about a fight in an apartment parking lot.

"Actually, we were called," Adrian replied.

"Sir, we had a call that there was a disturbance here in this parking lot," Mandy said. "Have you seen anything?"

"You're too nice to these jerkoffs," Adrian said quietly.

"Fight?" the man asked. "Nah, shit, I ain't seen no fight, but if you're looking for one, then stick around, pigs." He puffed his chest out and started to make a pig snort.

Mandy gave an unimpressed grin. "The complainant isn't outside," she said. "What was the address on that call, Rod?"

"Apartment 213, right where our friend here is standing," he answered.

Mandy sighed. "Of course. Of course it would be."

They started to walk closer, then in a flash the apartment door violently swung open. Another man came sprinting out of apartment 213 with a Louisville Slugger in his hands. The man who had been snorting was made silent by a bash to the head with the bat.

"Drop the bat! DROP THE BAT NOW!" Mandy yelled out, unholstering her gun. The man didn't drop the bat, but he did put it down to his side. He stood over the bloodied man he had just hit and started taunting him, though he was clearly beaten unconscious. "What, you think because the laws are here, I won't mess you up some more?"

Adrian darted toward them and pulled his Taser out. "My partner told you to drop the bat!" he yelled out, and after the man still didn't comply, he shot him with the Taser. Two prongs hit his torso and he yelped out like a dog, dropped the bat, and fell to the ground. Adrian put cuffs on him right away. "You're under arrest," Adrian said.

Mandy got on the radio. "Start EMS," she said, looking at the bloodied man on the ground.

"Adrian, you good?" she asked.

"Yeah, I'm good," he replied. "Did you start EMS? That guy looks rough."

Mandy stood over him. "Yeah. EMS is on the way. He does look rough. But he's breathing. No longer snorting at us, however."

"Ha," Adrian replied. He shook his head. "Not snorting at us now, for sure."

It was all only a few minutes, but it felt slower in the moment. Afterward, after EMS picked up the man whose head was beaten in with a bat, Mandy and Adrian took the man from apartment 213 to jail. They sat together in arrest review after he was booked, working on the report.

"I almost shot him," Mandy said. "And all I was thinking was, I don't want to shoot somebody today because I'm trying to get Ryan moved out here and I'm too busy for that crap."

Adrian laughed. "Well, glad it didn't come to that then. Because you're too busy to shoot someone."

"Just saying," Mandy said. "It's kind of funny that I almost pull my trigger and that is my thought process."

"Yeah, it is funny," Adrian replied.

She got quiet and began staring off into nothing.

"Jacobs? Hey—you all right?"

She took a minute to respond.

"I'm all right. I guess. Just a lot on my mind. You know, that cop in Houston—his family is getting death threats. All because he was doing his job, you know? I know the other guy didn't have a gun. But he was trying to strangle him with his own radio cord—you hear that?"

"Yes, of course I heard," Adrian answered.

"Yeah. He almost killed that cop. He was going to strangle him, but the cop shot him and killed him first. So, he lives. But now, now the media isn't telling the whole story, and they're making him out to look like a crooked cop or something. And his family is getting death threats. It's messed up."

"I know."

"This job, sometimes it's really stupid."

"Tell me how you really feel, Jacobs."

"Yeah. I know. But hey. We aren't in the news today, because you Tasered that guy before I could shoot him. And we're all right."

"We are all right. Just another fun day at the office." Adrian looked at her and raised his eyebrows. "You know, Jacobs, I came really, really close to shooting a guy two weeks ago, and I didn't even tell you the whole story."

"What happened?" she asked.

"So this guy runs a red light, right in front of me. I pull him over. Before I can do anything, I see him dive under his seat, reaching for something. Seriously I almost killed him right there in his seat. For real, Jacobs, I thought at first he was getting a damn gun. It was a flashlight. He wanted to get a flashlight to help him find his wallet, which was in his freakin' glovebox. When I saw the flashlight I could see in my mind how that would play out in the media. 'COP MURDERS MAN WITH FLASHLIGHT IN HAND.' Can you see it? Man, that would've been the end of me. You know?"

"Rod, I'm glad you didn't shoot the guy with the flashlight," Mandy said.

"Yeah, me too," he said.

Mandy smiled then. "Let's talk about something else. Who are you dating these days, Rod?"

"Jacobs, you won't believe me, but I'm still seeing Chantel."

Mandy's eyes widened and her mouth dropped. "Whaaaaaat? Chantel, the waitress? You mean a girl has lasted longer than a week with you? No way. Wait. Where's the camera? I'm being punk'd, right? Where's Ashton?"

"Ha, ha, Jacobs. First of all—that show ended years ago, so you need a new joke. Secondly, you and the rest of the shift have too little faith in me. I can keep a girl around. I just usually don't want to."

"Ah, but this one is different, I presume?"

"Well—yeah, you met her. You got a good impression, didn't you? I mean—you told me not to screw her over. I listened to you. You should be happy."

"Ha," Mandy laughed. "I am, Rod. I am happy to hear this. Chantel seemed sweet. Good for you, Rod. You're growing up, aren't you?"

"Don't tell anyone." He smiled. "So, what about you? How's Ryan? You said you're trying to get him moved here? For real this time?"

"Yeah, Rod, he's moving here for real this time," she answered. "So we're really good."

"Cool, Jacobs, that's really cool."

"Yep. I told him that I just didn't think I could do long-distance anymore. I told him we should just cut our losses, you know? And he said no, that he would do whatever it took for us to stay together. So he started looking at jobs here. He has an interview at the end of next week, actually."

"Good deal," Adrian said. "Look at us, Jacobs. A couple of responsible adults in healthy, monogamous relationships. Who'd have thunk it? Know what I mean? Ha. Hey, I know what we should do. We should double-date."

"Oh yeah?"

"Yeah. Let's plan it. I mean, after Ryan gets settled here and all."

"All right, Rod. We'll plan on that."

"Let's go ten-eight. Ready?"

"Ready."

CHAPTER 12

SHOW-UP THE NEXT DAY got started later than usual. It was the first time anyone could remember having to wait on Sergeant Torres to arrive.

"I'm telling you, it's because Sarge is leaving and ain't happy about it," Joe said as the shift was sitting around waiting.

"Zip it, Zavala, we don't know anything yet," Mandy said.

"Jacobs, why do you keep giving me grief when I try to talk about this?"

"Zavala, I don't like rumors. I don't do rumors."

Joe sighed. "Jacobs, I don't think this is a rumor. I'm telling you, I heard— "

"Exactly!" she interrupted. "You said you 'heard'—but probably not directly from him. Let him tell us."

"Jacobs hates rumors because she's usually the one they're about," White said from the back of the room. "Like, I heard you slept with half the shift."

"White, shut up," Chris said.

"What? Just saying—I heard a lot about her," Brian said.

"Shut your mouth, White," Chris said again, annoyed.

"White is an ass. But he has a point. Rumors bother me," Mandy said. "I've heard that I've slept with people that I've never even had seven with, so yeah—that probably has something to do with it."

Corey rolled his eyes at Chris and Brandon, all sitting together. "For real, this is where the conversation is going now?"

"Ugh. No. Just forget about it," Mandy said. "I just didn't want to hear a rumor being spread is all."

Corporal Harris walked in then. "Didn't want to spread what rumor?"

"Where's Sarge, Corporal?" Joe asked.

"Right behind me," he said, and then Sergeant Torres walked in.

"So, what rumor?"

Jacobs sighed. Zavala piped up. "There is a rumor circulating that Sarge is leaving the shift. Is it true?"

All eyes went to Sarge then. He gave a little head nod, and then said, "You guys are like a bunch of gossiping school girls. Pathetic. But yeah. Okay. I guess you should all know that I'm being pulled away. Transferring to Internal Affairs. Not yet, you still have me for a little while. I'm leaving sometime mid- to late April."

The air in the room was still. It felt like sitting among a crowd of fans whose team had just lost a big game. The shift respected Sergeant Torres—and trusted him. They had become like a family under his watch.

Perales was the first to speak. "That sucks," he said.

Sarge looked at him and smiled. "You'll get a new Sergeant, and you'll be just fine, rookie."

People started to smile then.

"Do we know who will replace you, Sarge?" Alex Mang asked.

"Nope. I'll keep you posted, children," Sarge answered. "Now. Harris—you read those BOLOs and let's all get to work."

"Yes, sir, getting on that now," Corporal said, getting the slide ready.

***

"IT'S NICE, YOU COMING and meeting me for lunch," Corey said to his wife.

"Lunch. You mean dinner? It's eight p.m."

"Well, lunch break for me. You know what I mean. I'm happy to see you."

"Me too. Thank God for my mom coming over to the house to put kids to bed for me. I needed an escape from that place."

Corey reached his hand out for Cassie's. "I know it can be a lot, staying home with them while I work these crazy hours. But I love you for it."

Cassie smiled. "I know you do," she said. "And I love you too. Especially in that uniform."

She winked at him.

"So, our shift will be changing soon," Corey said.

"Oh yeah?"

"Yeah—we found out today that Sarge is leaving. We don't know who's replacing him yet."

"Oh no—I love Sergeant Torres. I know you do too. Sorry to hear that."

"Yeah, I do like him a lot. The whole shift does. We've had a nice vibe in this shift, and I think it's because of him, you know? But that's the way it is. People move around, people move up. Which has me thinking."

"Thinking what?"

"Well, thinking that maybe it's time for me to try and promote. I think I'm ready. I think we're ready. Don't you?"

"Test for detective?" Cassie asked.

"Detective or corporal, yeah," he answered.

"Corey, I think that's a great idea, to go ahead and test. Definitely."

"You do?"

"Of course I do. You have my full support."

"I figured I would," he said. "Cass—you're the best, you know?"

She smiled at him. "I know. I can't believe I could be the wife of a detective or corporal soon," she said. "I didn't think you could get any sexier, babe, but I think you just found a way to."

Corey laughed. He patted his stomach, though his vest was in the way. "You still think I'm sexy even with this belly?"

"Of course I do," she said. "And what belly? If anyone in this relationship has a belly, it's me."

"No way," he said. "You, my dear, look incredible. Hot mom of three."

"Three I really hope are sleeping right now," she said.

"I'm sure they are," he said. "Now. What do you want to eat? I have a little over a half hour left and then I need to get back to the streets."

Cassie put her menu down and grabbed Corey's hand. "I just had a thought."

"Oh?"

"If you promote, we'll have more money, right?"

"Yes, that is part of my motivation to test, of course," Corey answered.

Cassie gave a sly smile. "Maybe if you promote, we should try for another baby."

Corey's eyes widened. "Really?"

"Really."

"Oh, babe, I would love to have another kid. I thought you wanted to be done though."

"I've been thinking about it more lately, Corey, and maybe we aren't done like I thought. I mean, let's see what happens with the exam. If you promote, let's try. You okay with that?"

Corey smiled and kissed his wife's hand then. "I'm more than okay with that."

***

AT THE END OF THEIR SHIFT, Danny and Corey were getting into their personal vehicles, parked side by side, at the same time.

"Perales, hey, I saw your girl at Starbucks last weekend," Corey said.

"Oh, yeah? You say hi?"

"Of course I did," he answered. "Cassie and I had all three kids with us, and we all chatted her up for a minute. She seems like a great girl. She gave my kids some cake pops. You two lovebirds still doing good?"

"We are," Danny said. "But this Houston stuff, she's been watching it all on the news, and it got her all worried about me."

"Well, if she's going to stay with you, she's going to have to find a way not to worry so much," Corey said. "Hopefully that will come though."

"Yeah—yeah, for sure. But . . . it's going to sound ridiculous . . ."

"What, rook?"

"In a weird, screwed-up way, it feels *nice* to have someone worry for me for a change. I haven't had that before."

Corey nodded and smiled. "Well, Sierra needs to stick around then."

"Yeah," Danny said. "Yeah. So, Hayes—things will be changing around here, huh?" Danny asked.

"Yeah, Perales, nothing good on a shift lasts forever," Corey said. "You'll learn that. People move around. Shifts change."

"I know," he said. "And I know it's only my first shift but I like it. I like Sarge. I was hoping it would stay this way for longer."

"Yeah, me too, Perales. This has been my favorite shift of my career so far. Anyway, have a good weekend."

"You too, Hayes."

CHAPTER 13

JOE, CHRIS, AND BRANDON WERE eating lunch together at Floyd's, a home-style-cooking restaurant in their district.

"Chicken fried steak for me," Joe loudly said. "That's where it's at, y'all. All day."

"You know what, Zavala, I think that sounds good. I'll have it too," Chris said to the waitress.

"Me three, please," Brandon said, handing his menu over to the waitress.

"So, Morgan, how's the family? How's Leah doing?" Chris asked.

"Oh, she's good, man. Did I not tell y'all my news?"

"We know she's knocked up, Morgan," Joe said.

"Yeah, Zavala, not that news. NEW news. Hold on a sec," Brandon said, pulling out his cell phone. He scrolled through his pictures and then held the phone out for Joe and Chris to see.

"I don't know what the hell I'm looking at, Morgan," Joe said.

"Oh, I do, I've seen an ultrasound photo a time or two before," Chris said.

"So, Janacek, what's the pic show?" Joe asked.

"Looks like a boy!" Chris answered. "Congratulations, Morgan!"

"Yes, it is a boy. My first son." Brandon smiled and put his phone back in his pocket.

"Hey, congrats, brother! Your first boy. Cool, man," Joe said.

"Very cool," Chris said. "And you'll be outnumbered now, like me and Kristin. When's Leah due again?"

"July," Brandon answered. "She's five months along now."

"Well, we'll buy you some diapers. And heck, man, I'll buy you some beer too. You'll be drinking more with the addition of another kid. Just trust me on that. I drink more and more with each kid."

Brandon laughed. "Well damn, Janacek, you have five kids. So are you telling me you're an alcoholic, or what? Should I worry for you?"

"Worry for yourself is what he's saying, Morgan," Joe said. "He's telling you to be afraid. Be very afraid."

They all laughed.

"Just messing with you, man," Chris said. "Three kids isn't any worse than two. But for real I'll get you diapers and beer before the baby comes."

"Yeah, I'll do that too." Joe said.

"Well, thanks, guys," Brandon said. "I know Leah will appreciate the diapers. And I'll never turn down free beer. So thanks."

***

"TOO. MUCH. CHICKEN FRIED STEAK," Brandon said to Chris as they were back in their patrol car, cruising their district.

"But damn good, right?" Chris said back. "Uh-oh," he then said.

Brandon looked forward and saw the broken taillight directly in front of him on a brown, early '90s model Chevy Silverado.

"Let's just give this guy a heads-up that he needs to get that fixed," Chris said, switching on his lights.

"Bravo 401, traffic," Chris said to dispatch on the radio.

"Go ahead," the dispatcher responded.

He read the plate and the guys got ready to approach the truck. Almost immediately, both Brandon and Chris were hit with a thick cloud of strong-smelling marijuana. Chris sighed in disappointment as he knew now this wouldn't be a simple "heads-up your taillight is out" call. He looked at Brandon and shook his head. Brandon had an expression that seemed to say "it is what it is" as he shrugged his shoulders.

"License and registration, sir," Chris said to the driver.

It was a young guy—nineteen, twenty maybe. His eyes were droopy. It was blatantly obvious that he was high, and as he reached over to open the glove compartment, a pipe fell out in plain view of both Chris and Brandon. Chris shook his head. "All right, step out of your vehicle," he said then.

"Dude, we just wanted to warn you about your taillight," Brandon said, putting cuffs on him and sitting him down on the curb. "Now we have to search your vehicle. Not smart, man, not smart."

"Come on, Officerrrr . . . give me a warning," the man said slowly. "Just let me go, man . . . please."

Chris and Brandon started to search the truck. They confiscated two pipes, one open package of rolling papers, and a dime bag of marijuana. They thought they were about to wrap up when Chris found a magnet intended to hold keys under the car with a bag of crack inside.

"Aw, great," Brandon said. "Good find, Chris. But dude, I wanted to get home on time. I'm too dang tired for this crap."

"I know," Chris said. "Dude's an idiot, riding dirty, high, with a broken taillight. Oh well. Let's get him to the jail, start arrest review."

***

"I CAN JUST TAKE THE GIRLS, I guess," Leah said to Brandon the next morning as he was reluctant to get out of bed.

"No, no, I'll get up," he replied. "I just need coffee. Strong coffee."

"Brandon, I've been trying to get you out of this bed for half an hour. Clearly you aren't ready to be up. It's fine. I can just take the girls to my appointment."

He sat up then. Put his feet over the side of the bed. Stretched, yawned—loudly—and stood. He kissed his wife's forehead.

"Nope. No. I've got it. Last time they went to the doctor's office with you, you complained about it for a week."

"Well, that was just because Ruby almost broke the stirrups in the office and I was mortified. This is just a quick checkup. I'll pee in a cup, get weighed, and they'll check the baby's heartbeat with a Doppler and then send me on my way. I can handle them for that."

Brandon shook his head and put his hands on his wife's shoulders.

"No, I'm up now. Sorry it took me a minute. It was a late night. Right before we were about to head back to the substation, Chris and I caught drugs on this guy. Couldn't let him go. Had to hang out at arrest review for a while. That's why I'm tired but I'm up now. Leah, I've got the girls. Go to your appointment. I love you."

She smiled at him. "Okay. Thanks, honey, for getting up. I'm sorry you worked late. I love you too."

***

LEAH PLOPPED DOWN ON A CHAIR in the waiting room of her obstetrician's office and looked to her right at the oak end table holding magazines for something to read.

The girl at the front desk had apologized to Leah, saying, "It's a longer wait than usual today, so sorry," but, if Leah was being honest, she was almost happy to hear that. She could sit in the waiting area and read a magazine in peace. No child climbing on her, no child calling for her to get up and do something. This waiting room, with the jazz playing on the speakers, beige walls adorned with huge floral paintings, and brown leather chairs, was her escape.

She picked up a *Parents* magazine with a picture on the cover of a chubby, smiling baby boy on it. She'd have one of those soon. She put her left hand over her belly. She smiled to herself, then felt a bit of panic. Her son was in there, kicking away, and that excited her. But it terrified her at the same time. Could she handle another baby? Three kids seemed like a lot. And with Brandon's crazy schedule . . .

"Mrs. Morgan?" the nurse called out. It was time for her checkup. She was almost disappointed.

"That wasn't a long wait at all," she said, putting the magazine back and getting up.

"Step on the scale, please," the nurse said.

Leah took a breath and stepped on. She raised her eyebrows as the nurse looked at the weight, looked down at Leah's chart, and said, "Only one pound up from last month . . . very good.

"Okay," the nurse then said, "take this cup for your urine sample, please."

Leah nodded, grabbed the cup, and headed to the restroom.

Later, as she sat waiting on the exam table for the doctor to come in, her thoughts drifted to Brandon. She felt guilty for having a bad attitude with him. He was tired, struggling to wake because of a late night at work—not a night of partying. She pulled her cell out of her purse and started to text. "I'm sorry you didn't get much sleep," she typed onto her cell. "I love you."

The doctor came in then.

"Leah, twenty-four weeks now, how are you feeling?" he asked.

"Pretty good," she answered.

"Good. If you have no questions or concerns, we'll just do a quick check of baby's heart rate and send you on your way until next month."

He put jelly on the Doppler wand and then rubbed it over her belly. The whoosh sound of the Doppler started. Leah smiled. Hearing the rhythm of her baby's heartbeat never got old.

"Good, strong heartbeat of one hundred forty-seven," the doc said.

She closed her eyes and felt gratitude for her son's heartbeat. She couldn't believe she would be giving birth in a little over three months. She imagined how her girls would act upon meeting their baby brother, and smiled again. As crazy as Leah's life could be at times, she knew it was good. Especially in that sweet moment, there on an exam table in a doctor's office, listening to a Doppler. Her emotions overwhelmed her and a single tear fell from her right eye.

"Everything appears to be right on schedule," her doctor said. He handed her a tissue and smiled at her. He cleaned the jelly off of her stomach with a towel and helped her to sit up. "See you next month."

The doctor walked out and Leah was getting up to leave too as her phone beeped. It was a text from Brandon. "Love you too."

CHAPTER 14

GABE TORRES SAT AT HIS kitchen table with a coffee mug in one hand, and the *Corpus Christi Caller-Times* in the other. His mutt, Rocky, was at his feet. He heard his front door open. He looked at his watch. Nine a.m. Eva surely wouldn't be coming home from work at this hour. Who was bugging him on his day off?

"Daddy, we're home," he heard. He stood up out of his chair as his two daughters walked to him, duffel bags in hand.

Veronica, his baby, approached him first. "Dad, did you forget we were coming home today?" she said, embracing him.

"Yeah, Daddy, you look surprised to see us," his older daughter, Victoria, said.

He kissed her forehead. Then his memory was sparked as the two girls said in unison, "It's Spring Break!"

"Ah," he said. "Of course. It's Spring Break and you're home from school for a week. I knew that. Your mother will be so happy to have you home this week."

They sat down together at the table. "I have a fresh pot of coffee, girls," Gabe said. "Would you like some?"

"Yes, Dad. As long as you have clean mugs for us," Victoria said, looking at his cup, which was stained from having not been washed in many, many pours of coffee.

Gabe shook his head and smiled. "You know we have other cups."

"How does it not drive Mom crazy that you won't clean your coffee mug, Dad?" Veronica asked, pulling out two clean mugs from the cupboard.

"Your mother met me when I was a sailor, girls, and she understands I hold on to certain Navy traditions."

"Yeah, but that's a weird one," Victoria said. "I bet she secretly is dying to wash that nasty thing."

Gabe shook his head. "So, how is school going?"

"Good," the girls answered in unison.

Gabe raised his eyebrows. "Just good? That's it? You girls had better be staying away from partying and boys. I want you both focused on your studies."

Victoria rolled her eyes. "Dad, you forget that I'm twenty-one now."

"And still a student," her dad replied. "And now watching after your freshman little sister as well. And you're both still my babies."

Victoria patted her father on the back. "We're both focused, Dad. Don't you worry."

"Yeah, Daddy, we're focused," Veronica said. "But we still have a little time for partying and boys on the side."

Gabe sighed and rolled his eyes as his girls giggled. "Don't worry about us," Victoria said. "Let's talk about you, Dad. Mom said something about you moving departments at work?"

"She did, huh? Yes. I'm leaving my patrol shift. Going to Internal Affairs."

"So this means you'll have regular hours, weekends, and holidays off?" Victoria asked.

"Yes."

"Oh wow," Veronica said. "I'm glad for that, Dad. I just kind of wish a move like this could've happened BEFORE we were both gone away at college."

The front door opened again then. This time, Eva walked in.

"Mom, you're home!" Victoria shouted.

"Of course I am, I took vacation," she replied. "I needed to be home with my girls for all of Spring Break."

"I had no idea that you took off," Gabe said.

"I told you, honey, you just weren't listening."

She embraced both of her girls as she put her oversized brown leather Coach bag down on the table.

"I just had to go in and clear out my inbox. But now I'm free the rest of the week."

"I'm so glad, Mom," Victoria said. "We missed you."

"I missed you girls too."

"Ma, we were just talking about Dad going to Internal Affairs," Veronica said.

"Yes, isn't it wonderful? I'll have your father around on weekends again."

"Yeah—but I was just saying it would've been nice if he had a gig like that while we were still home."

"Oh, please," Eva replied to her youngest daughter. "You don't know how lucky you are that he was only gone some weekends when you were growing up—and not for months at a time on deployment."

"Huh?" Veronica asked.

"You girls are too young to remember your father's Navy days, but those days—now THOSE days had some rough separations. Him working weekends? Nada compared to months away. We're so blessed to have your father when we have him. You have no reason to complain."

Gabe smiled at his wife. They had survived Navy life, infertility, the pain of waiting lists while adopting, and then finally, the struggle—and joy—of raising babies and toddlers, who in the blink of an eye had turned into college students. He knew, even when she was irritated with him, that Eva still had his back. She was Gabe's rock in an often unsteady world.

"I remember a little," Victoria said. "I was in first grade when Dad got out. I remember because the month after he retired was nine/eleven."

Gabe looked at his eldest then. "Yes, nine/eleven did happen the month after I retired. I remember that like it was yesterday. You were in first grade, and now you're a senior in college—how, my dear, is that possible?"

Eva raised her eyebrows at them and smiled. "Time flies when you're having fun, I guess," she said.

Veronica hugged her dad. "I'm sorry for giving you a hard time. Mom's right. I'm happy that you are going to Internal Affairs. You were—I mean, are, a great dad. And the hardest worker I know. I'm so proud to be your daughter."

"Ah, sweetheart, I am so proud to be your dad," Gabe said.

Victoria coughed obnoxiously, on purpose. "Suck-up," she mumbled in between fake coughs. "She wants a new car."

Veronica rolled her eyes and their parents just laughed.

"All right, girls," Eva said. "Come on back to your room with your bags. Let's get them unpacked."

CHAPTER 15

"DUDE, I SAW LOTS OF BOOBS yesterday at the beach," Adrian said to Danny at show-up the next day. "One chick, man, she was a ten. No joke. I thought about proposing right then, dude. A ten. Perales, you should come with me to the beach on our next day off, bro."

Danny just responded by shaking his head and laughing.

"What, you don't like boobs, Perales? Oh—I see. You've got a girlfriend now and can't do any Spring Break partying. I get it. Ball and chain. Yeah."

"Hey, Rod, maybe Perales is too mature for the drunk-ass college girls that are filling the beach this week," Mandy said. "Besides, shouldn't you be staying away from that too? I thought you and Chantel were exclusive."

"Rodriguez has something exclusive?" Danny asked.

"Hey, quiet, Jacobs, you'll mess up my rep."

"It hurts your rep to be in an adult relationship?" Mandy asked. "Come on now, Rod. That's ridiculous."

"Enough of that," Sarge said as he walked in. "And I'd like to think the beach isn't totally full of drunk college chicks—because my two daughters are home from school and with their mother at the beach as I speak."

That quieted the shift as show-up officially began.

"All right, with Spring Break being in full swing, you all know we have more visitors in Corpus than normal, and we will deal with all that normally comes with that. As usual, please try to get off on time, okay? I want to actually see my kids while they're here, so I'm taking off the next two days. Corporal will take care of you in my absence. Now—get to work."

Corey Hayes and Danny Perales ended up together on a deceased person call right after show-up. An old man had died in his house. A terrified Kirby salesman had rung his doorbell and noticed him dead in a recliner upon peeking in the front window. The old man looked stiff, he said on the 911 call. Upon their arrival the Kirby guy was still sitting on the porch steps. He stood up as soon as he noticed the patrol car had arrived.

"Officers, I think this man that lives here is dead, he sure looks dead anyway—and there is a weird smell when you get close to the door."

Corey looked at Danny. "Great. Already decomposing, probably. If you can smell it from the porch then when we get in it will be even worse."

"Sarge gave permission for forced entry," Danny said. "Let's get inside."

Corey kicked in the door, and the stench hit him in the face like a bag of bricks. He moved his head back a bit as if he was going to fall backward.

"Whoa," he said. "It's bad."

Danny's face scrunched up as he entered behind Corey. He coughed. "Oh, wow," he said.

"Yeah," Corey said. "This is a bad one." He coughed too. "All right," he said then, getting his composure. "Let's check the house, make sure no one else is here."

They searched each room, and then returned to the man in the recliner.

"See how purple that arm looks, the one hanging over the arm of the chair?" Corey asked.

"Yes, I see it," Danny said. "It's disgusting. Lividity, right?"

"Right. Blood is pooling up in that limb because of the way it's hanging over. Rigor mortis is starting to set in. Let dispatch know to page the medical examiner and homicide."

Danny radioed dispatch. "We'll look around for anything funny one more time," Corey said. "Then we wait outside. I don't want to have to be around this stench for longer than we have to be."

Nothing was found. No suicide note, no pill bottles, no alcohol. It was because they couldn't pinpoint a cause of death that homicide needed to be there, though they both assumed it was natural causes.

A few minutes later they waited on the lawn for the medical examiner and for the homicide detective.

"No big Spring Break plans, Perales?" Corey asked.

"Just hanging out with Sierra," he answered.

"Oh—right. How's that going, man? Still good, I assume?"

"It's great. I know it's only been a few months, but . . ." Danny paused.

"What is it, Perales?"

"Well, the shift is going to give me so much crap for this. You're the first one I'm telling. But I'm planning on proposing. I bought a ring and everything."

Corey patted Danny on the back. "Aw, man, that's awesome. Congrats, man."

"Oh, don't congratulate me yet, she has to say yes," Danny said. "But I do think she will. I just got her pop's permission this last weekend. I feel like I've known her dad my whole life, man. He's a good man. Finally one I can look up to. I didn't have my own dad growing up, but Sierra's dad, he treats me like a son already. It's really awesome."

"Glad for you, Perales. Really."

"Thanks, man. So, what about you, Hayes? Big Spring Break plans?"

"Relaxing, mostly," Corey answered. "My parents took our kids for the week. It's just me and the wife at home all week."

"Nice," Danny said. "So are your parents in the area and able to take the kids often?"

"They live in Dallas, but are actually looking to relocate here now that my dad is retired," Corey answered. "He just left the Dallas Police Department after thirty years. Now he and my ma want to be full-time grandparents."

"That's cool," Danny said. "I didn't know that your dad was a cop too. Law enforcement just runs in the blood, huh?"

"Guess so," Corey said. "I always thought growing up that my dad was the coolest dad I knew because he carried a gun to work. And I wanted to be cool like him. My mom tried to talk me out of this job—she's a worrier, you know, like most moms, I guess. She wanted for me to get a desk job, something safe. But I wanted to be like my dad. And I've never regretted following in his footsteps. He's a good man. Good dad. And was a good cop."

"That's cool, man," Danny said. "I gotta admit I'm a little jealous. I told you before, my dad wasn't around when I was a kid. It's nice you had yours and still do."

"Hey, Perales—you're starting your own family now, you know? With Sierra. By marrying her you're starting your family. You have a chance to build the family you wish you would've had."

"Yeah. You're right, Hayes. I do have that chance. Well, if she says yes. Ha. I'm excited. And blessed, really. To have Sierra in my life now. She makes me really happy, and gives me a new purpose."

"Always let her know, Perales," Corey said. "And you'll be golden. There's my marriage advice. Let your wife know how much you appreciate her even when times are tough."

"Ha, marriage advice on a dead guy call. Man. Happy to be working with you, Hayes," Danny said.

Corey laughed. "Yeah, dead guy calls bring out the marriage counselor in me, I guess. This time I won't charge you but next time we'll start a tab. Lots of good advice where that came from. Ha."

The homicide detective arrived then, and was followed shortly after by the medical examiner. They each made their rounds, checking around the house and checking around the dead body.

The medical examiner then called for body transport. While Corey and Danny waited on transport on the porch, an old woman came out of the house next door, saw the officers, and walked over.

"Officers, is Larry all right? I haven't seen Larry in over a week, maybe two. Oh, no, if you're here . . . he isn't all right, is he . . ."

Corey spoke to her first. "Ma'am, were you close to your neighbor?"

She shook her head. "Not really, no. I should have checked on him more though. Poor lonely man. He didn't have anyone to look after him. I could have made more effort. I have a grandson who comes and visits once a week, see ... I don't think Larry had anyone. Poor Larry. Can I go in his house, say goodbye?"

"Sorry for the loss of your neighbor, ma'am, but we have a medical examiner and detective inside, so we'll have to ask you to stay out here."

"Oh, of course. I understand. Thank you, Officers."

"Yes ma'am," Danny said to her, smiling.

The transport arrived then.

"And off he'll go," Corey said to Danny. "Sad, right? To end up dead and no one even notices for a while so your body starts to rot? If Cassie ever up and left me I'd eat my dang gun, man, rather than die alone."

Danny shook his head and laughed. "Me too, dude."

The homicide detective walked up behind them.

"Hey, gentlemen, wasn't there just a neighbor here, and you're out here coking and joking? Want to get keep it professional, get back to work, or clear out, or what?"

Corey rolled his eyes at Danny.

"We're about to go ten-eight, if medical transport is all done."

"They're wrapping up," the detective said as he walked back in.

"Literally wrapping up," Danny joked.

"Dude is uptight," Corey said. "Doesn't remember that he used to be us."

"Yeah," Danny replied.

They watched the medical transport guys roll the dead guy out in the gurney. His body was in a heavy-duty body bag.

"And now, we really will go ten-eight," Corey said as they walked to their patrol car. "Drive to the gas station, Perales. I could use a coffee."

"Will do, Hayes," Danny replied. "Coffee sounds good to me too."

***

"WOULD IT NORMALLY BE that fast, the process? I mean, I thought it was a really long time to get an adoption going," Chris Janacek asked Robbie Jackson as they sat down at a Subway sandwich shop for lunch.

"It can—and does—usually take a long time," Robbie answered him. "But Natasha and I are going through the state. And we weren't picky about age, race, any of that. And I guess we have luck on our side. No. Not luck, actually. God is answering our prayers. It's God's grace, Janacek. We're already being placed with a two-year-old little boy. A son. I'm going to have a son."

"Congratulations, Denzel," Chris said, standing up and hugging Robbie. They were in the middle of Subway with full gear on and some of the patrons were looking at them funny. Chris didn't care.

He was happy for his brother. "I'm so glad for you, man," Chris said. "I've been praying for you and Natasha."

"I know you have, brother," Robbie replied. "I know you have. Thank you, man." He wiped a tear from his eye.

They sat back down at their table and Robbie used a napkin to dry more tears. It became quiet as Robbie started in on his turkey sub and Chris opened his meatball sandwich.

Robbie looked up from his meal. "Janacek, I like you, but I will break in your house and murder you in your sleep if you tell anyone you saw me cry. Just know that."

Chris almost spit out a piece of his meatball sub. He had to quickly cover his mouth. Once he could finish chewing the food he nearly spat out and the roaring laughter that followed quieted, he wiped a tear from his eye.

"Dude, now I'm the one that's crying," Chris said, still laughing. "The former Army Ranger is threatening my life. Oh, man. Don't kill me, Denzel. I won't tell anyone that you've become a little girl who cries now."

"All right, well, I have to give fair warning," Robbie said, still chuckling.

"So," Robbie said after having a few more bites of his sandwich, "tell me something about fatherhood. You're like, a Superdad, right? FIVE kids? What advice you got for a rookie dad like me?"

Chris smiled. "I'm not a Superdad. I'm a Super-mediocre dad. But thanks to my Superwife, and my SuperGod, I manage."

"Okay," Robbie replied. "I've got a Superwife and a SuperGod too . . . what else?"

"Jackson, you're a good man and you'll be a good dad. Love your son. Love your wife. Love your God. You'll be just fine if you're doing those three things."

Robbie smiled.

"I can do those things," he said.

"I know you can, Denzel," Chris said. "Dude, you're going to have a ton of fun. Boys. Three of mine are boys. They're nuts, dude. But fun." He laughed.

***

After finishing up at Subway and going 10-8, radio dispatched a call out to an older residential area of their sector. 911 caller said they heard a woman screaming. Off Jackson and Janacek went, running code 3 with lights and sirens to find out what was going on.

As they were traveling there another call from dispatch came out—a burglary alarm was going off in the same area as the screaming woman.

Chris asked dispatch for more information but none was available. All they knew was that an alarm was going off in one of the homes, and a neighbor heard a woman screaming.

They arrived at the address given from dispatch and not a soul was in sight. Chris looked through the blinds in the front window of the house—the furniture looked ransacked.

"Hey, Jackson, looks like we may have something going on here," he said to Robbie.

They walked around the house to check the backyard. There was a swimming pool in the yard. Right away they saw a short, middle-aged man in what Robbie would later call "fancy" underwear (and nothing else) asleep out on a pool lounge chair.

"Dude has sequins on his skivvies," Robbie said quietly, trying not to laugh. Looking closer, they noticed he was bleeding from a cut on his arm and chest. They also noticed the back window had been broken and there was glass everywhere. As soon as Robbie approached him and called out "Sir," the man jumped from his sleep, obviously very startled, and accidentally fell into the pool his chair was adjacent to.

"You've got to be kidding me," Robbie said, as the man who fell in the pool was struggling. "Man. I don't want to jump in that damn pool."

"Neither do I," Chris said. He quickly looked around, clearly plotting something in his mind. He ran up to a pool strainer hanging on the fence and grabbed it.

"Really?" Robbie asked, starting to laugh.

"Well, you don't want to jump in, and neither do I, so yeah, really," Chris answered. "I'm going to scoop this guy out."

And Chris did just that, using a pool strainer. He used it to maneuver the little man to the side of the pool and Robbie was able to pull him out from there. As soon as Robbie had the man out, Robbie just shook his head while grinning. "I can't believe you just did that, but it worked."

The man was clearly on drugs. He wasn't making a lot of sense, but he did manage to tell Robbie and Chris, "I was attacked . . . with a, with a . . . hammer."

"We'll get you some medical attention, sir," Chris said as Robbie called on his radio for EMS. Nothing was making sense. They had to clear the house. Upon entering they saw more broken glass from the back window, a little bit of blood, and some broken drywall.

"Dude, it looks like *Predator Two* happened in here," Chris said, looking around.

Sure enough, there was a hammer on the ground. They also found hypodermic needles. They heard a television blaring upstairs; upon checking that out they discovered gay porn on a big screen. A toy Chihuahua ran out of a room barking and growling, looking as though it wanted to attack even though either officer could easily step on it and end its life. They tried to ignore it, though the dog became increasingly annoying.

A call came in from a cell phone lying on the ground. "LoverBoy" it read. "I'm going to answer it," Robbie said.

Chris raised his eyebrows and nodded as if to say, "Yeah, you should."

"Officer Jackson, Corpus Christi Police Department," Robbie said.

Chris watched him talk on the phone and do a lot of head nods and "uh-huhs" and eyebrow lifts. Then an eye-roll. "Sure you didn't. Of course," Robbie said.

After the call ended, Chris asked, "So?"

"So," Robbie responded, "his boyfriend says they did a little too much cocaine and things got out of hand. He admits to flailing a hammer around, but never hit him with it. He says. He obviously hit some parts of the wall. And he said he scared his boyfriend enough to make him run away from him and jump out the window, which made him scream, loudly."

"And that is the 'woman screaming' call from the neighbor, I presume," Chris said.

"Yes, looks that way," Robbie said. "And explains why the alarm went off."

"Wow," Chris said.

"Yeah, wow," Robbie replied.

"Cocaine. Explains a lot."

"Yep. Usually the unexplainable points to drugs of some kind," Robbie said.

"Is this the weirdest damn call or what?" Chris said.

"You're not kidding," Robbie said. "Weirdest call I've had in a while."

They couldn't help but laugh. "You just can't make these things up, Denzel, am I right?" Chris said later, writing the report.

"Nope," Robbie replied. "Sure can't."

***

COREY ENDED HIS CELL PHONE call with Chris, and Cassie couldn't help but ask why he had been laughing so much on the phone.

"Oh, Cassie, Chris was telling me about this call that I can't say I'm sorry I missed," he said. "It's a long story, but I was laughing because he told me that he used a pool strainer to get a guy high on cocaine out of a pool."

Cassie shook her head. "A POOL STRAINER? You guys are all completely crazy. My goodness."

He wasn't at work because on a whim he had taken vacation days so they could have a "staycation" with the kids and book a condo at the beach. Cassie had thought of it, and Corey had happily obliged.

"Babe, this is nice, being at the beach," Corey said to Cassie. "Thanks for setting this up for us. Kids are enjoying themselves, and so am I."

"Thanks for being the best husband ever and agreeing to a spontaneous trip," Cassie said. "I'm so glad your Sarge let you take vacation days on short notice too. This is nice."

And it was nice. They lay out on beach chairs soaking up the perfect April sun as their kids built sand castles. There wasn't a cloud in the sky, only endless blue as far as they could see. The wind was moving just enough to allow for a comfortable breeze. Corey closed his eyes and heard nothing but the splashing of the ocean waves and the hungry cries of seagulls passing over him.

"Ah, this is nice indeed," he said again to Cassie.

She felt proud of herself for pulling off a spontaneous family trip and smiled. She also thanked Groupon in her mind for the condo deal.

The kids had no idea. It wasn't planned out for very long anyway, but after Corey and Cassie loaded them up and told them they would be sleeping at a condo on the beach for a few days, they all three acted as if it were Christmas Day and Santa had brought them all exactly what they asked for.

"I don't have to make my bed for THREE WHOLE DAYS?!" Mackenzie had shouted. "Sweet!"

Cassie laughed. "That's what you're excited for, silly?"

"Not me," Jacob had said. "I'm excited for the beach."

"Me too," Noah added. "Maybe we'll see a shark!"

"I sure hope not, little man," Corey had said. "But I'm excited too. I'm excited for all of it. Fun family time will be good for all of us."

And as they were enjoying the beach, Corey couldn't help but smile to himself as he realized that it was, in fact, family fun time that they didn't know they needed. All was right in the world that day as they enjoyed the ocean breeze and the beautiful South Texas spring day.

CHAPTER 16

THE NEXT WORK DAY Brian White was on a call alone but called specifically for Alex Mang to meet him at the call.

Alex called Brian's cell phone. "You need me to twenty-five you, now? What's up?" he asked.

"I need you to translate for me, Mang," Brian answered. "I can't understand the woman talking to me here."

"Okay," Alex said. "She speaks Chinese?"

"Dude, something like that, just get here," he said.

Alex shook his head. "Brian, again, I'm asking you—does she speak Chinese?"

"I told you, something like that," he answered, clearly agitated at the question.

Upon arrival to the call Alex learned that it was a disturbance call, and that the woman Brian said he couldn't understand had called 911 after a fight with her husband.

"It never got physical," the husband said. He was sitting on the steps leading up to his apartment, smoking a cigarette. "I just yelled too much. Scared her. You can ask her yourself, she's inside."

"Your wife is inside," Alex repeated. He hoped she could speak at least a little English. Alex had learned some Chinese from his paternal grandparents, but used it so infrequently that he wasn't exactly fluent.

"Yes," the man said. "She's my mail-order bride. From South Korea. Not a great pick. But she's mine now, so whatever. Talk to her all you want. I didn't break any law, Officer. I can tell you that right now."

South Korea, Alex thought. *White thinks that all of us Asians are the same. Ignorant bastard.* Alex walked up the stairs and entered the apartment, where Brian was. "Oh good, you're here," Brian said. "You talk to the wife. I'll go back and talk to the husband some more. I don't see marks or anything on the wife . . ." Brian said, as he walked out.

"Hello, ma'am, my name is Alex Mang, and I'm also with the Corpus Christi Police Department," Alex said. "Would you like to tell me what happened?"

The woman was small and mouse-like. She had been crying. She looked up, hands folded neatly in her lap, and said, "I'm not sure why other officer call you. I speak English."

"I can hear that," Alex said. "So tell me what happened."

"My husband, he and I, we fought too much. I just was upset because he yell at me. I call nine-one-one but maybe should not have. I am sorry. I need to tell him sorry."

"Ma'am, are you sure you're all right? I am here to help you if you need help. Tell me the truth. Did your husband hurt you?"

She shook her head. "No, no. He never hurt me. No. My husband never hurt me. He never hit me anyway. I just get mad because he yell so much at me. Never hit me. Only yell. Time for you to go, Officer, please go. I am sorry for calling. I should not have called."

The call was wrapped up quickly after that.

"White," Mang said as they were writing the report, "you realize that she spoke English just fine, right?"

Brian shook his head. "Dude. I couldn't make out what she was saying. Like, at all. I figured you would be able to decipher what she was saying easier than me. And look, you did."

Alex sighed. "White—do you realize I am Chinese?"

Brian nodded. "Yep. Exactly."

Alex shook his head. "No, no, you still aren't getting it. I am Chinese. That woman in there was not Chinese."

Brian looked confused. "What? Are you sure? Because she sounded and looked Chinese, and I couldn't understand her, and then you came in and understood her just fine."

Alex sighed again and put his head back a bit. "Really, White? I really have to explain this? Okay. Dude, her English wasn't even that broken. She wasn't Chinese, either. She was from South Korea. Her maiden name was Kim, White . . . geez, man. Not all Asians are from the same country and speak the same language. You DO know that, right? Tell me that you know that."

"Oh, okay," Brian said. "Okay. I get what you're saying. So she was from South Korea and you're from China and they have different languages. My bad, dude! My bad. Shit. I wasn't thinking, I guess."

Alex lifted his eyebrows, lowered them, and then gave a tired grin. "Well, now you know." He didn't have the energy to argue further. "Not all Asians are the same."

"Gotcha," Brian said. "Gotcha."

***

AT THE END OF SHIFT that day Brian walked out to the parking lot at the same time as Alex. "I'm parked by you," he said when he noticed Alex looking behind his shoulder to see who was trailing him so close.

Alex didn't say anything, just gave a quick nod acknowledging him, and then threw his duty bag in the trunk of his car.

"Hey, Mang, sorry about earlier," Brian said. "I don't want for you to think I'm racist or something."

"Didn't really think that, White, just thought you were being a little ignorant," Alex replied. "But I'm over it."

"Okay, cool," Brian said.

Alex was starting to get into his car when Brian interrupted him by talking again. "Hey, Mang," he said.

Alex sighed and turned to face Brian again.

"Yep?" He was annoyed and ready to go home but trying to at least appear to be patient.

"I never got a chance to ask you. What was it like, shooting that old guy? At the farmer's market?"

Alex raised his eyebrows and pressed his lips together. Alex thought it was weird, White trying to be social all of a sudden. Normally he showed no interest in anyone other than himself. But okay, he would entertain the idea of White trying to talk, sure.

"Hm," Alex started. He closed his passenger door. He walked over to Brian's truck and put the bed down. "If I'm going to tell you what it was like, we'll have to sit awhile."

Brian smiled and joined him on the bed of the truck.

"It wasn't what I thought it would be like," Alex said. "You think about what it might be like to have to use your gun on someone, you know, in the academy, in training and stuff. But it's different when it actually happens."

"Different how?" Brian asked.

"Time is different. Every second feels like a minute during, but then it's over and it all felt like one second. That probably doesn't make much sense. But time was weird. Hard to explain, kind of. I don't remember even thinking in the moment. I knew I had to do it, and I did. Just like that. And for another—I thought I'd be affected differently, but I wasn't. It was just business. That sounds odd—that shooting a man was just business. But it was."

Brian nodded. "Yeah, just business, I can get that, man. I mean, I've never done it. But I can see what you're saying. Was it rough sharing that with your family? Or . . . wait. You're single, right?"

"Wasn't seeing anyone at the time," Alex said. "But telling my mom? Man. That was rough. She took it really hard. She hates that I'm a cop anyway, but now she worries even more. She wanted me to be a doctor. My dad did too, he's a surgeon, and I was supposed to follow in his footsteps . . . you know how the story usually goes. Anyway. They pretty much think my life is in danger every day I work."

"Ha, I mean, they aren't wrong," Brian said.

"I mean, you know how it goes, White," Alex said. "What we do isn't always scary. Some days I'm just going to calls where a Chinese speaker is requested and the lady doesn't even speak Chinese." He laughed.

"Dude, I know, my bad," Brian said, also laughing.

Alex was surprised that Brian had wanted to have a conversation, and even more shocked that he was enjoying it.

"You know, White, this is the first time we've sat down to talk, like, ever," Alex said.

"I know," Brian replied. "I know. The shift thinks I'm a dirt bag. I know my reputation. I'm not trying to change that, but I can try to talk a little more to y'all. So."

"So," Alex said. "What's new with you, White?"

White shook his head as he said, "Not much, man. My divorce has been final for a year now, so I'm finally starting to get out there, I guess, try to date again. I'm not good at the single life, like Rod is.

It's like I've forgotten how to talk to girls when I go out. So I just got this account on Match dot com. Is that pathetic, or what? There are some pretty girls there though. Man. Hopefully I meet a decent one."

"I have a cousin who met his wife on Match dot com," Alex said. "He keeps telling me to get on there too. I'm not good at the talking-to-girls thing either. I always tell him that I don't need that drama, but hey. If it works out for you maybe I'll finally try it out. This is 2017 after all. Online dating isn't what it used to be, right? It's cooler now?" He smiled at Brian.

"Dude, I hope that it's cooler now, because I've resorted to it," Brian said.

Alex nodded. "So." He looked down at his watch. "Man, White, I'm seriously tired. I'm going to go home. But I'll see you tomorrow, all right?"

"All right," Brian said. "Nice talking to you, Mang."

"Same to you," Alex replied. He opened his car door and was surprised to think he was being honest when he said that.

CHAPTER 17

MANDY WOKE UP FROM sleeping in way too late on her first day off. She almost felt guilty for sleeping in that late, like she had wasted away the first part of her weekend. After coffee she hit up the gym and tried to make the best of her day anyway. She awaited her call from Ryan letting her know his flight plans. He was to be in the next day, for his job interview there in Corpus Christi. She noticed her phone light up as it sat on the treadmill she was jogging on. New text from Ryan.

"Not coming in anymore," the text message read. "Sorry. I can't do this. I can't move and leave my life here. I know it isn't what you want. But it is what it is."

She slowed the treadmill down and then turned it off completely. She wiped the sweat from her forehead. She shook her head and read the text again.

You've got to be kidding me, she thought to herself. *Cold feet, again. And through text?! Really, jerk? That's enough. I'm done. I'm so, so done.*

She went into the locker room of the gym and briefly considered calling him. She wanted to tell him exactly how messed up it was to make her believe he was coming here and then just change his mind. She started to text him back, I CAN'T BELIEVE YOU ARE DOING THIS, and then stopped and deleted the words she had been typing. She threw her phone down. She was shaking from a combination of the run she had been in the middle of when she received his text, and her anger. She was livid. It would have to be over, really, this time. She was an adult, he was an adult. It was time to move forward. She thought they were finally doing that—moving forward—together. But now, she realized, she would need to move forward alone.

She went home from the gym and took a long shower. She considered calling a friend, but wasn't sure she wanted to share a sob story of what was looking to be like her failed relationship. It had been failing for a while, she admitted to herself.

Rather than sit in her apartment feeling sorry for herself, she decided she would go out. There was a new local bar in her neighborhood that she had been curious about. She could walk to it, even. It was a nice spring night, after all, and the weather was a perfect seventy-three degrees.

It was a bit out of her comfort zone, but she made up her mind to go. She couldn't think of a reason not to. She could have called a friend, but she knew it was short notice, and didn't want to bother with waiting for friends to get ready even if they were available. She just went.

Mandy looked casual. Her dirty blonde hair was back in a messy ponytail. She wore faded jeans with a slight tear in the knee and Converse tennis shoes. Her shirt was a light blue fitted tee that really made her blue eyes pop. Mandy was pretty without trying.

She was a bit nervous as she walked into the bar. It felt awkward to be going alone. She looked around as she sat. It was still early, so it wasn't very crowded. She noticed two middle-aged men playing pool. A couple was there, sitting at the bar, with eyes only for each other, lost in conversation. *I'll be sitting as far away from them as possible,* she thought.

There was a baseball game on the big screen behind the bar. She sat down and ordered a beer. Blue Moon with a twist of orange. The bartender, a woman not much older than Mandy, smiled at her and handed her the beer. "Want to start a tab, dear?" she asked her.

"Yes, please," Mandy replied, taking the beer and smiling back.

As she began sipping her beer she tried not to look as uncomfortable as she felt. She looked down at her phone. She reread the text from Ryan and then deleted it. Why should she be looking at that? Their relationship was as good as over.

Two younger guys sat down near enough by Mandy to where she could overhear their conversation. They looked to be just barely of drinking age. They were talking about their summer plans to float the Guadalupe River. She remembered making those plans herself when she was in her college years. It sounded really fun, actually. In her mind she imagined befriending these strangers—these fun-loving young guys—and tagging along on their adventures.

Then she wondered why that fantasy appealed to her to begin with. She wasn't a young college kid anymore. She wasn't old, either—of that she was certain. She was still hanging on to her late twenties. She was happily employed, doing the job she dreamed of as a child. What was missing? Was it that final commitment she craved? She'd hoped that Ryan would be the one. She looked at her bare left finger as she gripped her beer and took a long, slow sip. She set the beer down and sighed. She thought herself to be ridiculous for a moment—both to be imagining floating the river with some strange young guys she overheard at the bar, and to be so upset over her failed relationship with Ryan. She liked to think herself to be more independent than that.

She looked up at the big screen behind the bar again. She pretended to pay attention to the baseball game. Another man came into the bar and sat nearby her. Still, she had her eyes on the screen.

"Astros fan?" the man who just sat down asked.

She hesitated and made sure he was directing the question to her. "Oh, not really," she said. "I don't follow baseball all that much. But if it's on I guess I'll root for whatever Texas team is playing."

The guy smiled. His teeth were perfectly straight, she noticed. He held his hand out to shake hers.

"I'm Chad," he said.

"Hi, Chad, I'm Mandy," she said back, gripping his hand with hers.

"What brings you out to the bar this evening?" he asked. "Are you meeting someone here?"

"Long week, I guess," she answered. "No, not meeting anyone. You?"

"Same," he said. "Long week for me too."

She noticed then that his eyes exactly matched the hunter green color of his T-shirt. They were nice eyes, she thought.

"What do you do, Chad?" she asked.

"I'm in the Navy," he said. "Stationed here at the NAS."

"Oh, awesome," she replied. "What do you do for the Navy?"

"I'm currently attached to a training squadron, instructing pilots."

"Wow," Mandy said. "You know, I should've guessed you were military, with that high and tight hair cut you got there," Mandy said with a smile.

He gave a short laugh. "Yeah, pretty obvious, I guess. So, Mandy, what about you? What do you do?"

"I work for the city," Mandy said.

"Oh, yeah?"

"Yeah," Mandy said. "I'm with the CCPD. I'm a police officer."

Chad's eyebrows rose. "That's really cool," he said. "Do you like it?"

"I do," she said. "I really do."

He nodded. "That's great," he said.

She nodded back and smiled.

Suddenly she was more aware of her appearance. She wished she would have done her hair rather than just throw it back in a ponytail.

What was this that she was feeling? Was it an attraction to this Navy pilot, or a buzz from her Blue Moon she was nearing the end of? She couldn't be too sure.

Was this wrong? she wondered. No. No—no, she thought to herself. *I'm a grown-up. And a single one, at that. Ryan and I are over. I can talk to a cute guy at the bar and allow myself to feel something. I can do whatever I want. I'm single now.*

"So," Chad said then. "Have any cool cop stories to share?"

"Oh, geez," Mandy replied. "I have some weird ones, I suppose. Not sure about 'cool.'"

Chad smiled. "All right, share a weird one, then."

"Hm," Mandy said. "I have to think. Okay. Pretty recently I had to tase a guy who was on LSD. He was naked, and running down a street. He believed he was at a water park so he was occasionally trying to slide down the sidewalk."

Chad laughed. "No way," he said.

"Yeah," Mandy said. "Drugs make people do weird things. And we get called to settle them down. Fun stuff."

Chad shook his head. "Oh, wow, that is a funny one," he said.

She smiled at him. "All part of the fun of my job. You just never know what crazy you'll see from one day to the next."

"I can only imagine," Chad said. "I mean, just look around this bar and you can probably see some crazy stuff, right? Because of the drinking. I've been in here a couple of times since this place opened. Last time I was here, a drunk woman who looked to be, oh, I don't know, sixty maybe—was hula-hooping. And tried to get on top of a pool table and hula-hoop. I'm not even kidding."

Mandy laughed a little. "Oh, I believe you," she said.

"And that's just it—that's just here in this little bar. I'll bet you see crazier than that on the regular."

Mandy nodded. "I most certainly do see crazy," she said.

"And scary stuff too, right? I have to imagine."

"Yes, scary stuff too."

"Share one of those stories," he said. "Feed my curiosity. I mean, if you don't mind."

"Oh," Mandy responded. "You know what, Chad? I remember the funny ones more. Maybe it's a defense mechanism or something . . . but I remember the humorous calls and have no desire to retain the serious ones. So I don't have one to share, not at the moment."

"Okay. I get that. Of course. I hope you don't mind me asking. I just think it's so cool, what you do," he said. "Really cool. Thanks for your service to the community, Mandy. Sincerely."

"Hey, thanks for your service too," Mandy said back. "Sincerely."

She smiled at him again and this time felt that ping of attraction for what it really was as he smiled back. She lifted her beer to take a sip and noticed it was all gone.

"Need another?" Chad asked. "I'd love to buy you one."

"I'll accept," Mandy said. "I'm enjoying myself too much to leave just yet."

"Glad to hear," Chad said. "Because I am too."

***

"JACOBS, YOU DID NOT JUST tell me what I think you told me," Adrian said the next work day as he and Mandy were on patrol together. "You took a guy home? The same day you and Ryan broke up? Who the hell are you and what happened to uptight 'oh, I'm Jacobs, I have a long-distance boyfriend and I'm faithful and he's faithful and I'm uptight and I can't go out to the bar because I have a boyfriend' person I used to work with?" He had been elevating his voice to a higher pitch to emulate Mandy.

She punched his shoulder. "I wasn't that uptight, Rod, shut up," she said.

"Yes, Jacobs, you were," he replied. "But tell me more. I'm dying here. So who dumped who? What happened with Ryan? Didn't you just tell all of us that he was moving here?"

Mandy's face scrunched up a bit as she said, "Well, we didn't exactly break up, I mean I think it's implied, but we didn't officially say that . . ."

Adrian's eyes widened. "Whaaaat the hell, Mandy? You aren't even broken up and you took another dude home? That's messed up. You know that's messed up."

"Rod, we're over, for sure," she said. "But we just didn't say it exactly. He was supposed to fly in a few days ago. Had an interview set up, was flying in the final time—to move here. To move in with me. We'd been making plans. We talked about it once before, but he got cold feet—and this time, he really set up the job interview, and it seemed like he was a good fit for the job transfer, and it was all really going to work out this time. It was finally real. And I was happy. But then the day he's supposed to fly in, I get a text from him saying he can't do it. He can't move here. And he's sorry."

"Damn, Jacobs," Adrian said. "I'm sorry."

"No, don't be sorry," Mandy said. "I'm fine. Obviously, right? And by the way, Rod—not that it's any of your business, but I didn't sleep with Chad. He came to my place, we drank more on my couch, kissed a little, and both passed out. Honest."

He laughed. "Whatever you say, Jacobs. Man. Isn't it funny how times change? Now you're out playing the field and I'm one-on-one with Chantel. Funny how things work out."

"I know," she said. "Funny how things work out. That's for sure."

"And now, the guy you took home—you seeing him again, or what?"

Mandy. "I like him, actually," she said. "It's totally out of my character, just meeting a guy and letting him come to my place like that. But I don't know if I'll see him again. I mean, I need some time before I jump into another relationship, you know? But he's cute. And it was a fun night. He's a Navy pilot."

She smiled then.

"Oh, hell, Jacobs, snagged a Navy pilot, did you? Had some *Top Gun* fantasy going on or what?"

"If that's what you want to call it," Mandy said.

A call came through the radio then. A construction accident.

"It's too close by for us not to take it," Adrian said, reading the computer in their patrol car.

"Yeah, let's go."

Adrian hit the switch for lights and sirens on the patrol car and they sped that way. She tried to get ready for what she would see. She did that on the way to every call—tried to mentally prepare a bit, and formulate in her mind what she would do in certain situations. She knew a man had fallen and was presumed dead. She could handle that. She'd seen plenty of dead bodies since she'd been an officer. It didn't bother her. It did in the days before she was in law enforcement, of course. She could vividly remember her grandmother's open casket funeral when she was fourteen years old. She couldn't look at her grandma's dead body, and didn't understand at the time why anyone would opt for an open casket. She was so freaked out, then. But now? It was part of her job and she had no problem seeing the deceased. She could step over a dead body at a crime scene and grab a granola bar out of her pocket and eat it as if she were home on her couch. No problem.

They arrived and noticed right away the crowd circulated around what was obviously a dead man who had fallen from several stories up at a construction site. They knew it wouldn't be pretty, but it was worse than originally thought when they got closer.

"Oh, geez," Adrian said. "Jacobs. Get people back. Some guy is standing on parts of that dude's brain over there. Freakin' disgusting."

Mandy shook her head and started directing people to stand back.

"MOVIMIENTO, VOLVER!" she shouted. Her Spanish wasn't very good, but good enough, and the men started to listen to her and get out of the way.

"I didn't think we'd beat EMS," Adrian said to Mandy.

Just then the sirens were close enough to notice and they saw the ambulance heading their way.

"Good," they said in unison.

Corporal Harris pulled up then too, right behind the ambulance. He walked up to Mandy and Adrian.

"Was listening to radio traffic and close by," he said. "Honestly, I just wanted to come and see this. I heard he fell from pretty high up." He looked over at the dead man on the sidewalk. "Yep, this one is the worst I've seen yet. Yep. I was thinking it would be bad. Yeah." He shook his head lightly but his face was indifferent.

"You can't even see a head at all on this guy," Adrian said. "Just pieces of his brain everywhere. Freakin' mess, for real. I'm glad we don't have to clean this up."

"No joke, Rod," Mandy said back.

"Well, you two have this, right?" Jared said.

"Yes, Corporal," Adrian and Mandy said in unison. They watched him as he walked back to his patrol car.

"Seriously, he's always as cool as a cucumber, am I right?" Adrian said.

"Yeah, he is. You can never see what he's thinking. He's the calmest dude I know."

They were able to clear out shortly after EMS arrived. It was obvious that he accidentally fell, and no one else was injured.

Getting back in the patrol car, Adrian looked to Mandy and said, "Jacobs, I'm starving. Time for seven yet?"

Mandy lifted her boots one by one, checking to be sure she hadn't stepped in any of the brains that were on the sidewalk of the construction site. She looked down at her watch and nodded at Adrian. "Yes, Rod, it is actually time to eat. I'm hungry too. Let's go ten-seven. Where do you want to eat?"

CHAPTER 18

"HEY, WOULD ANYONE BE interested in an Easter egg hunt in my backyard this weekend?" Chris asked the shift after show-up. "The wife wants to organize something for the shift kids. And I can get some beer for those of you who don't have kids but want to come over anyway and hang out."

"Sounds good to me," Brandon said.

"Yeah, Cassie will want to help out, I'll have her call Kristin," Corey said.

"Cool," Chris said. "It's on then. This Saturday, be at my house any time after twelve. I'm planning to order a bunch of pizzas. We'll do lunch, let the kids hunt for eggs, and drink some cold ones."

"Thanks for the offer, Janacek, Natasha and I will come for sure. That way the shift can meet our boy," Robbie said.

"Hey, that's right, Denzel is no longer just a ridiculously good-looking police officer who gets hit on by the women we take to jail, he's now a father!" Chris said with a laugh. "Congrats, brother."

"Hey, that's right, congrats, Jackson," Brandon said. "That's awesome."

Mandy got up and hugged Robbie. "Congrats, Jackson."

Joe gave him a high five. "Congrats, brother."

"Yeah, congrats," Danny said from the back of the room.

"Thank you, everyone, thank you so much."

"What's your boy's name, Jackson?" Corporal asked.

"His name is Jayden. He's two."

"We should be having a party for you and Natasha," Mandy said then. "Like a shower or something."

"No, no, we don't need that," Robbie said. "My wife's family had a little get-together for us already and bought us a ton of stuff. Spoiled already by his grandparents, I'll tell you that. Thank you for the offer though."

"Well, I'm bringing you a gift anyway," Mandy said. "For Jayden. He's two, you say? I can buy a gift for a two-year-old boy. I have a nephew that age."

"Thanks, Jacobs. That's nice of you."

Sarge walked in then. "Jackson, congrats on the kid," he said.

"Thank you very much, sir," Robbie said.

"No problem. I heard you all are having an egg hunt. My kids are grown but I'll be there. Janacek—your place, correct?"

"Yes, Sarge," Chris answered. "This Saturday."

"I'll bring the wife. It'll be my last time getting together with you all. You'll have a new sergeant here next week and I'll be in Internal Affairs."

It was quiet then in the room. Almost awkwardly quiet.

"Well, we knew it was coming, and I'm leaving next week, no need to get weird about it," Sarge said. "Get to work now. Be off on time. All right? All right."

***

JOE ZAVALA WAS ASSIGNED to a 911 call that had come from a mother who was complaining about her thirteen-year-old son. He arrived to the address on the call and found a woman in her mid-thirties crying on her porch. She saw Joe walk up and stood up off of her step.

"Officer Zavala, Corpus Christi Police Department," Joe said, walking up to her. "You called us?" He could see a curious face peering out from inside the house at the front window.

"Yes, Officer, I need help with my son," she said, wiping tears from her face. "He won't listen to me."

"Is that your son I see peeking out the window now? He won't listen to you?" Joe asked, waiting for more of a reason why he would be called out there.

She turned around and looked sternly at her son through the window. Her face seemed to be telling him *you're in trouble now*. She turned back around and nodded at Zavala, but said nothing more.

"And . . ." Zavala said, waiting again for more.

"And . . . I am needing some help from you."

"Help getting him to listen to you?"

"Yes. He is thirteen. He won't listen to me. I need him to help me around the house, Officer. I told him to put the trash at the curb and he refuses. Absolutely refuses. And me, look at me, I'm a small woman. I can't force him. But you can."

Zavala shook his head and took a deep breath. Then he began to talk to her again. "Ma'am, unless you are wanting to tell me that your son did something of a criminal nature, I'm going to have to leave."

"No, no, please—please. He isn't doing anything criminal, I know. But can't you help me anyway? Can't you make him listen to me? Please. Just go tell him to take out the trash. Please. I need your help."

"No, ma'am, I'm not going to do that. I'm not going to go tell your son to take out the trash."

"Why not?" she asked.

"Because if I do, that takes away YOUR power as a parent. You go tell him to take out the trash. And if he refuses, discipline your child. It is *your* responsibility."

With that, Joe cleared the call and left. He was agitated, but it wasn't the first time he had a call from a parent who just wanted help parenting. It certainly wouldn't be the last.

He went on break with Mandy and Alex. They sat at Whataburger and talked through their mouths full of burgers and fries. "I left, I told her no," he said to Alex.

"Good for you, Zavala," Alex said. "I've stopped helping those people too. Once I held an eleven-year-old while his dad spanked him. So stupid. It's not our job, man. I wish those calls would stop coming in."

"No joke," Mandy replied. "We can't fix in thirty minutes what years of crappy parenting has done. I hate those calls too."

"So, you two making it out to Janacek's house this weekend?" Joe asked Mandy and Alex.

"Planning on it," Alex said.

"Me too," Mandy said. "I don't want to miss the last get-together with Sarge before we get the new one."

"For real," Joe said. "That's why I want to go too. Hey, you two know our new Sarge?"

"I know him," Alex said. "He's a douche."

"I heard that too," Mandy said. "Trey Johnson is his name, right?"

"Right," Alex answered. "I worked with him when I was with an FTO still in District Charlie. No one likes him. Like, not a single damn person likes him. I don't know how he ever got his own shift."

"Sucks that he's coming to ours," Joe said.

"It does suck," Alex replied. "For real."

Joe got up from the table to order a chocolate milkshake after finishing his Whataburger. He didn't ask Mandy or Alex if they wanted one too, he just ordered them each a shake anyhow. He walked the three shakes over to the table, and they sat at their booth in Whataburger, quietly sipping their milkshakes, until their lunch break was over.

***

"EASTER EGG HUNT TIME!" Matthew, Chris and Kristin's seven-year-old son, yelled as he heard the doorbell ring on the day of their Easter party. He ran to the door holding his Easter basket. Kristin yanked it from his hand as she walked toward the front door. "Not quite yet, buddy, but soon."

"Awwww, Mommy, I want it to be now," he said.

"Just be patient," she said, and she opened the front door. Cassie was there holding grocery bags in hand. Corey and their three kids were right behind her.

"Cassie, hello, and welcome," Kristin said, reaching in for a semi-hug as Cassie's hands were full.

"Thanks, Kristin, I come bearing gifts of filled eggs to hide and some cookies."

"Great, thanks so much," Kristin said. "Follow me to the kitchen and we'll start getting ready to put eggs out together. I still have some to fill."

Chris walked to the door as Corey was walking in too. "Hey, brother," he said to Corey. "Hi, kids, welcome to my house," he said, looking at Jacob, Mackenzie, and Noah.

Corey smacked Jacob lightly on the head to get his attention. "Say hi to Mr. Chris," he told him.

"Hi," the three said in unison as they walked into the house.

"Sorry to crash the party early," Corey said to Chris as the kids ran upstairs. "Cassie said she needed to be here early to help. She always feels like she needs to help organize things like this."

"Oh, Kristin told me that Cassie was helping her by bringing eggs and helping her hide them before we got started, so no big deal," Chris said. "Besides, I could already use a beer. Want one?"

"Heck yeah, I want a beer," Corey answered.

Chris handed him a Dos Equis. "Lime?" he asked.

"Nah, I'm good. Thanks."

"No problem, man," Chris said. "So. Hayes. How was your time off? You guys go somewhere?"

"Oh, we stayed close, Cassie booked us a condo on the beach at Port A. It was good though, man. Nice to have a little time off, relax at the beach, that sort of thing. Kids loved it too."

"Sweet," Chris said. "Yeah, I think I'm going to do something similar soon, if I can get Kristin on board. We could use a day or two out of the house too. Especially these crazy rugrats. They need to get out too."

"Well, it's a good time for it, not too hot yet," Corey said. "You should do it sooner rather than later when it's a hundred damn degrees outside."

"No joke," Chris said. "Yeah, I'll talk to Kristin more about it. Get something on the calendar."

The doorbell rang then. Matthew ran downstairs again and grabbed his Easter basket that Kristin had placed back on the kitchen table. "Easter egg hunt time!" he yelled again.

"Nope, sorry bud, still not exactly Easter egg hunt time," Chris said. "But I promise you we'll let you know when it is."

"Awww, Daddy," he said, sulking. "I want it to be egg hunt time right now."

"Not yet, Matthew. Go play." Chris opened the door. This time it was Brandon Morgan and family.

"Hey, Morgan, welcome," Chris said.

Kristin and Cassie walked to the door. "Leah, you look adorable!" Kristin said, walking over to give Leah a hug.

"Oh, please, I'm as big as a house!" Leah said, waddling in.

"Mommy has a baby in her tummy," Grace said, trailing behind her parents.

"Yeah, it's a brother," Ruby added, the caboose walking in with her family.

"Well, I think that is really cool that you are going to have a baby brother," Kristin said to the girls. "Grace, Ruby, feel free to set your Easter baskets down at the kitchen table and head upstairs. That's where the kids are playing until we have our egg hunt."

The girls were happy to oblige and hurried up the stairs.

"Leah, Cassie and I are just about finished filling eggs in the kitchen, want to join us?"

"Yes, I do want to join you," Leah said, and she followed the ladies to the kitchen as Brandon followed Chris to the living room.

"We've started drinking already, care to have one?" Chris asked Brandon.

"Of course I would like to have one," he answered. "I'll have several, probably. Got a pregnant wife in there and her hormones are all over the place. I'm walking on eggshells these days. It's stressful." Brandon looked behind him toward the kitchen. "Crap, you don't think she can hear me, do you? I'll be in more trouble if she knows I'm talking about her."

Corey laughed. "No, bro, they can't hear you. But keep it down to be safe."

"They're busy gabbing," Chris said. "I know Kristin is anyway. That woman can talk."

The rest of the shift began to arrive little by little to the Janaceks' home. Alex showed up with a six-pack of beer to contribute and some homemade guacamole with tortilla chips.

"I didn't know you could make guacamole, Mang," Corey said.

"What, because I'm Asian I can't make a Mexican dish? This entire shift is racist," Alex joked. They both laughed it off.

Joe and Gloria Zavala were the next to show up. They brought nothing but their loud voices. "Always so good to see you all," Gloria said, walking in. "Kristin, tell me what I can do to help."

"Just keep us girls company," Kristin told her. Gloria was happy to join the ladies in the kitchen.

Corporal and Sarge showed up at the same time.

"Uh-oh," Chris said as he opened the door. "Supervisors are here at the same time. Should we be worried?"

"This was not planned," Sarge said. "Corporal is just obsessed with me and clearly following me."

"That's what it is, Sarge," Jared joked. He puckered his lips out and formed a frown then. "I should be following you because you're ditching us and I'm just so sad."

Becca and Eva just stood by their husbands, shaking their heads. "Hey, do I see Max hiding behind you?" Chris said to Jared.

"You do," Jared answered. "Max, why don't you get in there and play with the other kids?"

"They're all up those stairs," Chris said, pointing to the stairwell.

"Mommy, can I go play?" Max whispered to Becca.

"Of course you can, buddy," she answered him. "I'll hang on to your Easter basket. Go have fun." As Max made his way to the stairwell Becca looked at Chris and said quietly, "He's a little shy at first, but he warms up quickly."

Chris just nodded. "Well, everyone, come on in," he said. "Egg hunt will be on soon, ladies are hanging out in the kitchen, and I'm starting beer number two in the living room."

"Beer sounds good," Jared said, following Chris.

Robbie Jackson, his wife, Natasha, and their son, Jayden, arrived next. It was the first time anyone on the shift had met Jayden. Robbie looked proud as Chris opened the door to welcome them inside.

"Jackson, good to see you, brother," Chris said, shaking his hand. "Nice to see you again, Natasha," he said then to Robbie's wife, giving her a hug. "And this guy—I don't believe I've met you before, little man," he said as he kneeled down to Jayden's level. He put his hand out to shake Jayden's little hand. "You must be Jayden. Nice to meet you, buddy. Welcome to my home."

Kristin walked to the front door from the kitchen. She couldn't hide her excitement. She had her hands up to her mouth. "Oh, my," she said, rushing up to hug Natasha. "So this is little Jayden. Congratulations, Natasha! Congratulations, Robbie!" Kristin hugged Robbie as well. She looked at Jayden and then took him by the hand. "Hey, Jayden, would you like to play with my kiddos? I can show you where they are. We have a playroom upstairs." She mouthed to Natasha—*This is okay, right*? Natasha and Robbie nodded yes in unison, so Kristin continued to walk Jayden upstairs.

Everyone there started congratulating Robbie and Natasha one by one.

"Thank you," Robbie said. "Thank you to everyone. Jayden is a dream come true. We appreciate all of your prayers and well wishes as we've gone along the way. Really. Thank you all so much."

"Yes, thank you for all of the support you've given us," Natasha said. "I am so grateful for Robbie's work family. For all of you."

They split up then, the ladies returning to the kitchen, the men returning to the living room.

By the time the ladies were ready to hide the eggs for the children, the entire shift had shown up, even Brian. "He's been coming around more, at work," Leah mentioned to Cassie shortly after he arrived. "I heard he hasn't been such as jerk lately."

"Well, I guess that's good," Cassie said. "He's still a little off to me though. Right?"

"I know why now," Leah said quietly. "Brandon told me the low-down on his divorce. Apparently it's not what we all thought it was."

"Really?" Cassie asked. "The rumor was that he left his wife because she was overweight, right?"

"That was the rumor," Leah answered. "But it isn't true. He opened up to Adrian one night, and then Adrian talked to Mandy about it, and now I think almost everyone knows what he told him."

"Which was . . ." Cassie waited.

"That his wife left him, it wasn't the other way around."

"Huh," Cassie said.

"That isn't all," Leah said.

Cassie just looked at her, waiting.

"She left him for a woman. She's a lesbian."

"Oh, wow, I never would have guessed that," Cassie said. "Geez. I guess that has to be hard when your spouse up and leaves you for someone of the same sex. Yikes. Oh, wow. I can see why someone would be jaded after that."

"That's what I'm saying," Leah said. "I feel bad for the guy. I know he's been rough around the edges, but I get it. And Brandon says that he really seems to be making more of an effort to talk to people at work now."

"Wow, I'm surprised Corey didn't mention anything to me," Cassie said. "If the whole shift knows the truth now and all."

"Probably just hasn't come up yet is all," Leah said. "Brandon seriously just mentioned this to me today on the way over. I was asking if the whole shift was coming, and when he said yes, I asked if that included Brian, and then he just started spilling what he heard."

Cassie nodded. "I see. Well, okay then. That is quite a story."

"All right," Kristin said, walking up behind them holding bags full of filled plastic eggs. "Who is helping me put these in the yard? Kids are all upstairs still, correct?"

"Correct," Chris yelled out from the living room.

"We're helping," Cassie said. "Actually, Leah, go sit in the kitchen. Kristin and I can handle this."

"I'm fine," Leah said. "I'm not dying, just a little bit pregnant."

"Just a *lot* bit pregnant," Brandon said from the couch with a grin on his face.

"You hush," Leah said, waddling outside to help hide eggs.

"You have a death wish, Morgan?" Corey said. "Pregnant women are homicidal, dude."

The guys laughed and continued to enjoy their cold beers. The women actually enjoyed spreading candy-filled eggs in the back yard, adding some along the Janaceks' playscape and in their garden.

The pizza was delivered as the ladies were hiding eggs. Shortly after that everyone was spread out throughout the house, eating pizza, enjoying themselves.

Then after lunch was finished, all of the shift-mates who were parents had their cell phones out, on camera mode, snapping pictures as the shift kids ran outside to collect their eggs. Even Jayden, the newest shift kid, was having a good time as Natasha helped guide him to find eggs. Chris and Kristin's youngest, Benjamin, had taken a liking to Jayden and stayed close by him during the egg hunt.

"Benjamin is two years old too, Denzel," Chris said. "So looks like he and Jayden are new friends."

Robbie smiled. "Yes, looks like they are," he said. He continued to snap pictures of Jayden with his Easter basket as it was slowly filling with eggs.

"You're going to learn the real fun of Easter is the sugar crash that will come later," Corey said, slapping Robbie on the back. "And then you'll learn that is why us parents, we drink."

Robbie laughed. "Well, if that's the case at least I have you experienced parents to drink with."

"You aren't just giving him the horror stories, are you?" Cassie said to Corey. "Come on. You can't be scaring him yet. Give it a little time."

"Oh, he may as well be told the truth now," Corey replied. "It's all good though. My rugrats are already opening eggs and eating candy, see?" Corey pointed to his oldest, Jacob, who had a mouth full of Skittles and his hands opening more eggs to see what other goodies he had collected.

"I'm getting him," Corey said as he set his beer down. He went up to Jacob and snatched his basket. "Dad, come on, that's mine," Jacob said.

"You'll have to catch me first, son, then I'll give it back!" He ran, basket in hand, up the slide of the playscape.

Jacob laughed and ran after his dad. Mackenzie saw what was happening and yelled out to her younger brother, "Noah, look at Daddy! Let's get him!"

Five-year-old Noah had a hilarious, clumsy run but made it to the top of the playscape where his dad was, just after Mackenzie had run up there. Jacob had already tackled his dad and they were going down the slide together.

"Good thing we opted for this heavy-duty playscape," Chris said to Kristin. "Hayes would've broken it by now otherwise."

All three Hayes kids were on their dad at the bottom of the slide then, in the grass, rolling around, trying to pin him down. He was too strong for them. He managed to get all three of them down on the grass, and one by one was tickling them. The kids' faces were red from laughing so much. It was a sight.

"My crew is crazy," Cassie said to Leah as they watched from the porch.

"Yeah, but whose isn't?" Leah said. "Oh look. Ruby opened some chocolate already. So much for her new Easter outfit."

Cassie looked over and saw three-year-old Ruby covered in melted Twix bar.

"Seriously, it's mini-size," Leah said. "How does she manage to make that huge of a mess with a mini-size piece of chocolate?"

"It's a mystery I'll never solve," Cassie said. "But hey, I'll help her get cleaned up." Cassie walked over to Ruby and snatched her up. "Let's go inside, Rube, and wash some of this candy off of you so you can continue to play. Sound good?"

Ruby smiled at her and had chocolate-covered teeth as well. Leah laughed. "Cassie, thank you for cleaning up my mess of a child."

"Oh, no problem, Leah!" Cassie said, walking inside.

Kristin walked over to Leah, who was still watching Corey tickle his kids. She smiled at Leah. "We have a great group of people here. Our husbands are lucky to be on this shift. Am I right?"

Leah smiled back. "Oh, for sure," she said. "You're totally right. By the way, Kristin—great party. All the kids are having a great time, and I've enjoyed myself. I know Brandon has too. Thanks for putting this all together."

"I'm happy to do it," Kristin said. "I enjoy these sorts of things."

"I think we're heading back inside for a bit," Chris said, walking up to Kristin and setting his hand on her back. "Getting a little humid, right? I want to go sit in the AC. Kids are fine to stay out back awhile."

"That sounds good," Kristin said. She looked back over to Leah. "Leah, want to come back in? Sit down awhile?"

Leah rubbed her belly. "Yes, baby says yes, we should sit down. Maybe eat another piece of pizza too."

Sierra was in the kitchen getting herself seconds as well. Leah noticed as Sierra lifted the lid of the pizza box that she had a diamond on her left ring finger. "Wait a minute . . ." Leah said, making it obvious the ring had her attention.

"Sierra . . ." Leah said. She looked at her, eyebrows raised, waiting for a confirmation.

"Well, it took long enough for someone to notice," Sierra said. "Danny! Where are you?"

Danny walked into the kitchen from the living room. "Here. What's up, Sierra?"

"Danny, someone finally noticed," Sierra said.

"Noticed what?" Robbie asked, walking in from outside and joining the conversation, Joe trailing behind him, holding Jayden.

"This," Sierra said, as she held up her hand.

"Ah, no way," Robbie said. "Congrats, brother. Congrats, Sierra. Welcome to the fam." He hugged Sierra and gave Danny a high five.

"Perales is getting hitched?" Zavala said then. "Awesome, man. Congratulations."

It was a train of congratulatory hugs, high fives, handshakes, and one slap to Danny's rear end from Adrian after that.

"So, how did he ask?" Mandy said then to Sierra. "I can't see Perales as anything but the rookie. Hard to imagine him as a romantic."

"Oh, he is really romantic," Sierra said. "But I don't want to embarrass him. Danny, you want to tell the story?"

"No, you can," he answered.

"Okay then. Well, he took me to Water Street Seafood Company."

"I love that place! Did you get oysters on the half shell? We always get oysters on the half shell, don't we, babe?" Joe said to Gloria.

"Babe, let her finish the story," Gloria said to Joe, with a wink. "And it's my turn to hold that cutie pie," she said, taking Jayden from Joe. She sat down and began a game of peek-a-boo with him.

"My bad," Joe said. "Right. I won't interrupt anymore. Sierra, tell us the rest."

"Well, that is where we had our first date. Yes, we did get oysters on the half shell, Joe." Sierra was grinning from ear to ear. "He seemed quieter than normal. I knew something was up. He was sweating like crazy."

Some of the guys started laughing.

"Then it just happened. We didn't even have our oysters yet, actually. We had just ordered them. Our drinks came, and then right after the waiter left from setting drinks in front of us, he said he had an important question to ask, and of course I had a feeling of what that question was."

"Hope he got down on one knee," Sarge chimed in.

"Yes, he did. Right there in the restaurant, people watching and all. He got down on one knee and said the question was 'will you marry me?' . . . And well, you all know that I said yes." She smiled and looked down at her ring.

"Awww," Leah said. "I can't believe I didn't notice your ring until just now. And I really can't believe none of your shift-mates did, Danny. What the heck, Bravos? *No* attention to detail. *None*."

"Oh, I saw it earlier," Brandon said.

"Yeah, so did I," Brian said.

"Why didn't you say anything?" Kristin asked them.

"We figured rook would tell us when he was ready," Brandon said.

The guys nodded in agreement.

"Okay, okay. I guess that makes sense. Well, congratulations again, you two. I'm so happy for you both."

Everyone settled in different areas of the Janacek home. Some kids were outside, some had run back upstairs to play. A couple of the little ones ran around the living room. Kristin leaned against her kitchen island and looked around. Everyone appeared to be having a good time. *Successful gathering,* she thought to herself. Even Brian White was being social. She was happy to see that. He was normally off, alone in a corner somewhere, or absent altogether from the shift gatherings.

Chris went and put his arm around Kristin. "Nice party, babe," he said. "You did a good job."

"Oh, I had plenty of help from other wives," she said. "But thanks, honey. I'm glad we did this. It's been fun. You having fun?"

"I am, yes," he said, looking over then at Gabe and Eva. "And this is Sarge's last party with us, you know? He's gone after next week."

"I remember you telling me," Kristin responded. "I'm sorry he's leaving. I've always really liked him, and Eva is really sweet too. I'll miss seeing them at these get-togethers."

"Yeah," Chris said. "Me too."

CHAPTER 19

BRIAN AND ALEX ARRIVED within a minute of each other to a domestic dispute in the worst part of their district. A woman was standing outside a duplex smoking a cigarette. She wore a McDonald's uniform, shirt untucked, and was barefoot.

"Oh, shit, you have got to be kiddin' me," she said, seeing them pull up. "Who called the laws out here?"

Then her husband walked out. He had an open cut on his forehead. "Me. I called 'em," he said.

"Officer Alex Mang, Corpus Christi Police Department," Alex said to the man. "Do you need medical services, sir?"

"Nope, just wanted to make a report with y'all."

"Ma'am, I'm Officer Brian White, CCPD—explain what happened here today," Brian said, standing in front of the woman.

"No, nothin' happened," the woman said. "We all right. Nothin' happened at all."

"She's lyin'," the man said. "She did this to me. This cut on my forehead, my wife gave it to me."

"You shut the hell up," the woman said.

"No, no, I will not shut the hell up," the man said. "She got mad and hit me over the head with a pipe, Officers."

"You're gonna get us both arrested, you dumbass," she said, flicking her cigarette away. Brian walked over and stepped on it, using his boot to put it out.

"Well?" Alex said, cueing the man to tell the rest of his story.

"Well, my wife worked today, and I had the day off," he started.

His wife interrupted him. "Day off? DAY OFF? You're unemployed, dumbass. I'm the breadwinner 'round here. Don't act like you had no 'day off,' don't act like you have a damn job. I'm the one out workin', not you."

Brian's attention shifted back to the husband. "Sir, do you want to continue telling us what happened?"

"We had some crack here at the house. It was *both* of ours, not just hers. I smoked it. Smoked all of it. On accident. I didn't mean to smoke it all. I didn't realize I'd done that, honest. When she came home, she wanted some. I told her it was all gone but I'd get some more later. She got really mad then, really mad. Got crazy. And you see this?" He pointed to the cut on his forehead then. "She cracked the pipe over my head."

The woman stood there, arms crossed, shaking her head. "Dumbass piece of shit," she said. "Dumbass piece of shit!" She started to sprint over to him them. Brian was able to stop her, quick, and get cuffs on her.

"Ma'am, you should know we aren't going to stand here and watch you attack your husband," he said, walking her over to the patrol car. "You're under arrest."

The husband watched on as his wife was being arrested, arms crossed across his chest, back straight, as if proud. He had a smirk on his face.

"Dude, crack is illegal," Brian said to him. "But . . . next time, maybe share? Maybe your wife won't assault you."

Alex shook his head. "White, don't encourage him," he said with a laugh.

"Not encouraging him," Brian replied. "Just sayin'. Share. Have manners. You know?"

Alex had to laugh, but tried to keep it to a minimum as he opened up the back door to the patrol car and guided the woman into the back seat.

***

ON THE OPPOSITE SIDE of the Bravo district, Mandy and Danny were taking a call together. A man had called requesting help but then hung up on the dispatch operator as they were asking for further details. They knew his location—he was in a vehicle parked along the water at Ocean Drive, near the south entrance of the naval base. He had given the description of the vehicle he was in, but he had never said what he needed help with.

"Red Ford Ranger, single cab—that's our guy," Mandy said as they pulled up along the truck. They got out and saw the man sitting in the bed of the truck, facing the water.

They approached and immediately Mandy could tell the man was crying. Sobbing, actually. Big fat tears. His nose was a snotty mess.

"Officer Mandy Jacobs, CCPD," she said, walking up slowly to him. "This here is Officer Perales. Can we help you, sir?"

He wiped his nose with his shirt. He looked toward the water, but not at them.

"Sir, I believe you called for help?" Danny said then, as the man wasn't answering them. The man looked back down at his lap. His shoulders were drooped down. He had a look of defeat. He looked up at the sky, then out toward the water again. Finally he looked over at Mandy and Danny.

"We're here because of a nine-one-one call that was placed by you, we believe," Mandy said. "But we can't help you unless you talk to us."

The man's crying calmed down and he sighed. He appeared to be in his late twenties—early thirties, maybe. Skinny white man with dark black hair and bushy eyebrows. He had an unkempt goatee and wore a Star Trek T-shirt.

"I called, yes," he said. "But then I decided maybe I shouldn't have called. Officers, I am beyond your help. Worthless, that's what I am. I think I'm just going to end it. There is no other solution."

He looked back out at the water. Tears began falling again.

"Call for a mental health officer," Mandy told Danny, quietly. "Tell them we've got a suicidal subject."

"Who's the MHO on our shift?" Danny asked.

"Zavala is. I think Mang is too," Mandy said. "Call on the radio and see who can get here."

As Danny was calling on the radio, Mandy walked a little closer to the man. She looked at him.

"What's your name, sir?" she said. She figured she needed to get him talking.

"Nathaniel," he answered.

"Nathaniel, where do you work?"

"Flour Bluff High School," he said. "I teach algebra. My students, they don't respect me though. Even they can see me for what I am. Totally worthless."

"Gosh, Nathaniel, you don't look worthless to me," Mandy said.

"I am," he said. "Can I talk to the male officer now?"

Danny overheard that and walked over. The man looked at him. "Can I just talk to you, Officer . . ."

"It's Perales," Danny answered him. "My name is Officer Perales. And of course you can talk to me."

Zavala is en route, Danny mouthed to Mandy. She nodded to acknowledge him and then stepped back a bit, as Nathaniel had requested to speak to Danny. She tried to give them some space but looked on.

"Officer Perales, you married?" Nathaniel asked.

"I'm engaged," he answered. He waited for more from Nathaniel, curious as to where he was going with this.

"So you have a girl. You won't get it probably."

"I can try to get it, if you'll let me know what 'it' is," Danny said. "Tell me what's on your mind."

"Officer Perales, I want to end my life because it's pathetic," Nathaniel said. He wiped his nose with his shirt again. "I'm a thirty-year-old virgin. Yep. It's true." He whimpered then. "No woman will have sex with me."

Danny's eyes widened. He wasn't sure what to say. He looked over at Mandy, who had obviously heard what was said. She averted her eyes as he looked at her and tried to look serious, though she wanted to laugh.

Danny shook his head. "You know, Nathaniel, that doesn't make you pathetic at all," he said. "I'm sure the right girl just hasn't come along yet."

Mandy smirked at Danny then. Danny looked at her as if to say, *What? What else should I say? Help me!*

But she wasn't helping. He walked closer to her and whispered, "Why that face? Did I say something wrong? Why don't you come talk to him?"

"Because he asked to speak to a male," she answered quietly. "Besides, I'm having fun watching you try to handle this one."

A patrol car came up then. "Ah. Our MHO is here. Sweet," Mandy said.

Joe stepped out of the vehicle. He walked up and Mandy told him what they knew so far.

"All right, if he seems like he's for real, I'll transport him to a mental health facility so they can keep an eye on him," Joe said before walking over to Nathaniel. "But hey—Perales—you should've just told him to go pay for sex. Get it over with so he's not a virgin anymore."

Mandy punched his shoulder. "Zavala, please," she said. "Tell me you aren't condoning prostitution."

"Kidding!" Joe said. "Only kidding, promise. I've got it, guys." He softened his face then, as if he were an actor entering a new scene on a stage. He walked over to Nathaniel then and began talking to him.

"And that is why if you get qualified as an MHO you get a little extra pay," Mandy said to Danny as they were entering their patrol car. "You have to deal with crazy crap like that."

They drove away after Officer Zavala took over the call. Mandy's cell rang. She looked down at the screen, thinking it was her mother, who would occasionally call her to check on her while she was working. She was surprised to see Ryan's number. She had deleted the contact, so his name wasn't popping up, but she knew that number.

"You gonna answer that?" Danny asked. "You look funny, Jacobs. Who is it?"

She tried to come out of the trance seeing his number had put her in. "Oh. Oh. It's my ex, actually. Not sure if I should get it or not."

She couldn't hit the answer button. Just couldn't. So she let it go to voicemail. *Why would he be calling?* she wondered.

"You good, Jacobs? Want to talk about it?" Danny asked.

"I'm fine. Thanks for asking, Perales. I'm okay. Just weirded out. Not really expecting to hear from him anymore, you know?"

Her phone beeped. A text, this time. "Miss you. Call me."

Her eyebrows rose upon reading it. "Oh, for crying out loud," she said under her breath.

"Him again?" Danny asked.

"Him again. Texting me. It's just weird. He's so wishy-washy. I seriously think I'm just going to ignore it."

"That's what you want, to ignore it?" Danny asked.

"Yeah. Yeah, I'm sure of it. I was with him long enough, gave him enough chances to make me a priority, you know? He didn't then and now that we're really through he does this. I'm fed up. I don't owe him anything, so yeah. I'm sure I want to ignore it."

"Well okay then," Danny responded. "If you want to talk about it, I'm here."

"Thanks, brother," she said.

"Anytime, Jacobs."

She smiled and deleted Ryan's text message. She was sure she didn't need to respond. She was surprisingly enjoying her newfound singledom. She felt free to do what she wanted to do. She figured when the time was right for her, she'd enter a relationship again. But it wasn't going to be with Ryan. He was in her past now, and was staying there.

Her phone rang again. "Seriously?" Mandy said, but then she looked down and saw that this time, it was her mom. She let out a sigh of relief.

"Just my mom," she said to Danny. "I can answer this one."

"Hello?" she said. "Oh, hi, Mom . . . Yes, I am at work. It's fine. Just came from a call . . . Oh, some guy wants to hurt himself, but it's all handled now."

She grimaced. "I'm not riding alone currently, Mother. But I do, often. And I'm fine."

Danny watched as she was listening to her mother and rolling her eyes. "No, really, Mom, we've had this conversation too many times. I have work to do, so I'm going to let you go. Yes, I am staying safe. Always."

She said her goodbye and hung up her cell phone. "My mom doesn't trust I can do my job," she told Danny. "Not sure she ever will. I've wanted to do this since I was a kid, and she knows that. But she always kind of hinted, without saying out loud, that police work is work for men. Not for women."

"Sorry, Jacobs," Danny said. "If it's any consolation at all, you're one of the best officers I know. I like riding with you."

"Aw, thanks, man," Mandy replied. "Dude, I'm lucky. Ever since I started with the Bravo 400s I've never felt like I needed to prove my worth here. Like, not because I'm a female. I did feel like I had to prove myself as a new officer, but not as a female. So I'm a lucky one, I think."

CHAPTER 20

"TODAY'S THE DAY," Alex said to Chris as they walked into the substation on the new Sarge's first day with the shift.

"It is," Chris said. "Big change for the Bravo 400s today. Guess it was time for that though."

"Guess so," Alex responded.

They walked into the show-up room and there was Sergeant Trey Johnson, the new leader of their shift.

"Gentlemen, welcome to work," Sarge said, shaking their hands.

Chris reached out to shake his hand. "I'm Janacek," he said.

Alex followed suit, putting his hand out. "Mang," he said.

"Nice to meet you both," Sarge said. "Surely you know by now that my name is Sergeant Johnson. Please take your seats."

They quickly followed his instruction and sat down. Sergeant Johnson was a big man. Fit, but big man. Looked like he could bench-press the both of them if he wanted to. His head was bald and shiny, and his teeth were too bright. They almost looked fake.

Joe and Adrian walked in together next, and as always, Joe was laughing too loudly as he came in.

"No freakin' way, Rod," he was saying as he walked in the room. He saw the new Sarge standing there, arms crossed across his chest, and he settled his laughing down.

"Oh, hey," Joe said, shaking Trey's hand. "I'm Zavala." Adrian was right behind him. Joe said, "Behind me, this is Officer Rodriguez. We were just cokin' and jokin', Sarge, didn't mean to barge in all loud and shit." He smiled.

Sergeant Johnson looked unamused and did not smile back, but he did sternly shake both of their hands. "I'm Sergeant Johnson, nice to meet you both."

Another minute went by. Shift-mates trickled in one by one, shaking the hand of their new supervisor before taking their seats. Usually there would be chatter as they waited for show-up to begin, but today, it was silent. You could hear the ticking of the clock on the wall. Adrian shifted around in his seat. Joe tapped his foot on the carpeted floor and swayed a bit, as if a song were playing and he was going along with the rhythm. Alex twiddled his fingers. Chris chewed his fingernails. The ticking of the clock seemed slower than normal. Finally, as everyone else had arrived, and they hit 2:30, Jared stood in the front of the room and began talking.

"Bravo 400s, today we welcome our new shift supervisor, Sergeant Trey Johnson, to our shift. Let's all give him a warm welcome."

The shift applauded.

Jared looked around at the shift, and then looked at Sarge. "I just want to say, we're happy to have you here leading us. So, welcome again, Sergeant Johnson."

"Well, thank you for that," Trey said. "I've met you all now, so we don't need to do introductions again. Please sit, Corporal," he said and Jared obeyed, quickly taking his seat back.

"I've worked with Corporal Harris before, I'm glad to be doing that again." He looked at Jared again then and Jared responded with a head nod. "I also worked with your previous sergeant, Sergeant

Torres, before. I know he was very well liked and I understand why. I'm expecting under the leadership of Sergeant Torres and Corporal Harris, you've got a squared-away shift and this pleases me. I don't have much to tell you about myself, but I'm sure we will all get to know each other better as the time goes by. For now, I just want to say hello. So. Hello."

Trey looked around at everyone and finally gave a half-smile. "Well then. All right. To work we shall go now."

The Bravo 400s couldn't wait to get out of that room. The air was too stiff in there. It was hot and humid on that spring day, but it still felt freer than when they were inside the building with the new Sarge.

"Maybe he isn't that bad, just doesn't make great first impressions," Mandy said to Adrian as they headed out.

"Guy could smile a little," Adrian responded.

"He did, kind of, at the end, I think . . . right?"

"That was a smile? That's the face I make when I take a crap, Jacobs. That wasn't a smile."

Mandy laughed. "Ew, Rod," she said as they parted ways and entered different patrol cars.

"You know it's funny," he said.

***

ALEX AND ROBBIE TOOK a family violence call together. A couple had been fighting. No kids were present, which made it a bit less stressful than many of the family violence calls they had become accustomed to.

Alex started talking to the woman, and Robbie started talking to the man. They had to separate the two, so Alex was outside while Robbie stayed in.

"So, what happened?" Alex asked her. He watched her intently as she began telling her side of the story. She was a pale-skinned girl and he noticed right away the grip marks on her wrist. It was obvious her husband had put those there. He didn't notice any other marks, however. He was looking for them as she spoke.

"He hit me on the face, Officer," she said. "He's always trying to control me. He didn't like that I had a night out with my girls. So he hit me."

Again, he looked but saw no marks on her face. "Okay," Alex responded. "Was it an open hand or a closed hand that he hit you with?"

"I don't know," she said, looking down. It was clear she was having to think of what to say next. "Um. Close-handed. Yeah."

Alex was writing things down as she spoke. "Okay, close-handed," he said back to her. "How many times did he hit you? Did he hit you anywhere else?"

"Um, how many times?" she repeated. "How many times? I don't know. Six, maybe. Yeah, like six times."

"He punched your face six times? With a closed fist?" Alex asked. She was a small woman, with pale skin. Her husband was a big man. If he really hit her on the face, even once, there would be a mark of some kind.

"Yes, about six times," she answered.

"Okay," Alex said. "How did you get those marks on your wrists?"

"Oh, he grabbed me," she said, then noticing the marks herself as if she hadn't known they were there before. "Yeah, he grabbed me hard and it hurt. Still hurts."

"Looks like it," Alex said. "Ma'am, I have to ask, because clearly you have the marks on your wrists, but I see no injuries on your face . . . Are you sure he punched you in the face six times?"

She crossed her arms and tilted her head. "Why would you ask me that? You think I'm a liar?! Are you kidding me? I want to see your supervisor, Officer."

Alex remained calm as he spoke to her again. "Ma'am, I just have to ask these questions, okay? For the report. I have to ask a lot of questions because when this goes to court we have to have plenty of details. I'm just doing my job and trying to help you."

She uncrossed her arms then. "Whatever. Okay."

Inside the house, Robbie was getting a different story from the man.

"Officer, she just came home from what she told me was a night out with her girls, but I know she's cheating on me," he said. "I called her out on it and she flipped out. She started slapping and threatening me, went all crazy. Scratched me up some."

Robbie saw the marks on him right away. His face was a purplish-red across his left cheek. He had scratch marks on his face, neck, and arms. One nail gouge was so deep on his arm that it was bleeding.

"Did you ever hit her back?" Robbie asked.

"No. I didn't hit her, not one time," he answered, very matter-of-factly. "I grabbed her wrists and shoved her away. I wasn't trying to hurt her though, just wanted to get her off of me. First time I shoved her, she ran back to me, so I shoved her back again. That time she ran out the house and told me she would call y'all and say that I was the one hitting her so that you'd take me to jail. I stayed, because I know the truth and have nothing to hide."

Alex left the girl waiting out front and he talked everything over with Robbie.

"Seems pretty clear cut who the aggressor is," Robbie said.

"I agree with you, Jackson," Alex responded. "I'm going to hook her up. We need to get a victim statement from the husband. I'll go get the paperwork."

He walked back outside and saw his new supervisor, Sergeant Johnson, talking to the woman.

"Oh, I'll make sure we take care of him, ma'am," Trey was saying. "Also I'll get you a counselor out here."

He noticed Alex walking up to him then. "Officer Mang, call victim services out here for Mrs. Clark, here. She needs to speak to a counselor."

Alex couldn't hide the confusion on his face. He turned around and walked back in the house.

"Hey, Jackson," he said. "Our new Sarge is out there talking to ol' girl."

"Huh?" Jackson asked. "Why?"

"Dude, your guess is as good as mine. He's asking me to get a counselor out here. I was just about to arrest her."

Robbie shook his head. "No. No, let's go talk to him."

Outside again all three were standing in a semicircle discussing the call.

"Sir, Mang and I have assessed that Mrs. Clark is actually the aggressor, not her husband. We've spoken to both of them, and if you look at the injuries, they actually align with Mr. Clark's statement, not hers."

Trey shook his head. "No. I disagree. I believe she is the victim. You need to make an arrest."

Robbie looked at Alex, then back at Sarge. "Sir, I really feel strongly about this one that our assessment is correct. I don't mean to disrespect you, however . . ."

Trey cut him off. "However, that is what you're doing right now. Now, Officer Jackson, you are to go in there and arrest Mr. Clark. That's an order."

Robbie had a confused look. He looked at Alex again. Alex had taken a deep breath and then shrugged his shoulders.

With a defeated look, Robbie looked at Trey again as he was about to walk back inside. "Okay, Sarge. I'll go hook him up."

"Good," Trey responded. "I didn't want to have to write you up for insubordination. Now, Mang, did you call for victim services yet?"

"No, sir, but I'll do that now," Alex said.

"Very well," Trey said. "Good work, gentlemen."

Robbie walked back in and was glad his Sarge was still outside. He was shaking his head as he walked up to the husband. "Mr. Clark," he started as he was pulling cuffs out, "trust me when I tell you, I really don't want to do this."

The husband saw the cuffs and got confused. "I thought you agreed with what I told you," he said. "Why are you arresting *me*?"

"Because my sergeant is making me. I believe you, I do. I was given a direct order to do this. But, look, man, I'm sorry. I really am. Believe me. Look, you can fight this case, and you should. I'm writing a detailed report for you. Okay? Fight this charge."

He walked him out to put him in the back of the patrol car, right past the wife, who had a huge grin on her face. She flipped him off as he walked by. He didn't respond, just kept his head down as he was placed in the back of the patrol car.

"This is some bullshit," Alex said to Robbie after Sergeant Johnson had left the call.

"Yeah, it is," Robbie responded. "Sergeant Torres would've never come and taken over a call like that. Never. He wouldn't have sided with that liar, either."

"Yeah. I know. Guess we're seeing firsthand now why everyone calls him a squirrel."

"Yeah. Freakin' sucks."

***

CASSIE LOADED TWO BOXES packed full of baby boy clothes in the back of her SUV and headed to Leah's house. She had promised some hand-me-downs once Leah found out she was having her first boy. She stopped by the grocery store and bought a large box of Pampers as well.

Leah opened the door and was surprised to see the big box of diapers sitting on her porch. "Cassie, you didn't have to do this," she said. She hugged Cassie's neck. "Gosh. You're seriously the best."

"Well, I think it's crap that you won't let me throw you a shower. So I'm just going to have to bring gifts sporadically, I guess, until July. And maybe after he's here too." She picked up the boxes and walked into the house.

"It's my third baby, I don't need a shower," Leah said. "But thank you for the offer. It's sweet. You're too good to me."

"Third baby, but first boy. It would have been totally fine to have a shower."

"I guess so," Leah responded. "But I feel like I have what I need. Seriously. And look, thanks to you, I have more than enough. You sure you can part with these clothes?"

Cassie smiled. "Oh, I kept some. I haven't told you yet, but Corey is taking the next test and we both agreed that if he gets promoted, we'll try for baby number four."

"Oh wow, Cassie, that's awesome!" Leah hugged her again. "In that case I don't want to take any of your clothes though."

"No, no, I have so much, please take these," Cassie said. "I want to give them to you. I'm just super excited. I can't believe it's May already. Short two months and your little man will be here. Hey, did you and Brandon agree on a name yet?"

"Not yet, no," Leah said. "We're thinking it will come after we see him for the first time. We have a short list, but just haven't been able to set one in stone yet."

"I get that," Cassie said. "In fact, NONE of my children were named until after their births. So I totally get that. I was the same way. Had to see them first, too."

"Hey, are you hungry for an unhealthy snack?" Leah asked, smiling. "Brandon bought me a dozen cookies from Tiff's Treats. Snickerdoodles. Want one?"

"Um, what kind of person would I be if I turned down a cookie?" Cassie said. "Of course I want one."

The pair of them walked into Leah's kitchen. She grabbed two snickerdoodle cookies out of a box on the island and they sat down at the kitchen table to enjoy them.

"It's not normally this quiet in your house, Leah," Cassie said. "Where are the girls?"

"Oh, Brandon took a day off today, and he's spending time with them."

"That's sweet," Cassie said. "Just because?"

"Yes, just because," Leah answered. "We just had to register Grace for Kinder the other day and it made him realize just how little time he'll have with her if he remains on evenings after school starts in August. He had some 'Daddy guilt,' he said. It was bad enough to make him take a day off and spend it all with Grace and Ruby. He took them to the museum, said after that they were going to get some ice cream."

"Aw, what a good daddy," Cassie said. "And it's true—the evening shift takes away from the kids. On school days that are Corey's work days, he's asleep while the kids are getting ready for school in the morning, and by the time they get home, he has already left. So he only sees them on the weekends, and when he works weekends, it's only for a few hours in the morning before he goes in."

"That's hard," Leah said.

"It is," Cassie responded. "Cop family life sucks sometimes. But, since he's getting ready to take the promotion exam, I'm thinking all of that could change. I'm hoping he gets detective. Can you imagine? A nine to five job, banker's hours? It'd be so awesome. I'll be doing cartwheels if he gets promoted to detective, for sure."

"Doing cartwheels and doing the baby making," Leah said, giggling.

"Ha," Cassie said. "Yeah, I guess we'll be doing the baby making too if he gets detective."

"Well, that's awesome that he's testing, Cassie," Leah said. "I hope he gets it. That would be so amazing for your family."

"Thanks. So, guys' camping trip is in two weeks," Cassie said. "Brandon is going, right? Corey booked a campsite at Lake Corpus Christi State Park."

"Oh, yes, he is going," Leah said. "He offered to stay home because I'm so pregnant. But I told him he should go. It's not like I'm going into labor anytime soon, I still have a little over eight weeks to go till my due date. He always has fun camping with Brandon. I'm glad they've remained friends for as long as they have."

"Ditto," Cassie said. "It's nice for them too. A weekend away, fishing, drinking beer. I was thinking while they are away, you and the girls can have a slumber party at my house. I've got a million kid movies, and Pinot Noir for me, and I'll get ice cream for you . . ." She smiled. "I know ice cream isn't as good as Pinot, sorry. But one of my post-baby gifts for you will be a bottle, I promise. Then we'll do a REAL girls' night! Well, unless I'm knocked up then. Then maybe I'll be the driver while you have a fun night."

Leah laughed. "Ice cream will be just fine," she said. "And that sounds great. Girls will love that. We'll plan on it."

"Good," Cassie said. She looked down at her watch. "Oh. I have to go get Noah, he's at my mother's house but she has a doctor's appointment. Then of course I need to be home for the bus stop."

"Your mom okay?" Leah asked.

"Oh, yes, she's fine," Cassie said. "Routine appointment. Nothing out of the ordinary."

Leah gave a little head nod. "Ah. Okay. Thanks for stopping by, friend, and for the baby clothes and diapers. I really appreciate it."

"Hey, no problem," Cassie said. "And I'll see you in a couple of weeks."

"Sounds good," Leah said, hugging her. "Bye."

"Good-bye, friend," Cassie said.

CHAPTER 21

"TELL ME THERE'S SOME WAY to switch him out, Corporal," Alex said to Jared in the parking lot before work. They'd arrived at the same time, parked next to each other, and Alex had just shared the story of the family violence call Sergeant Johnson had taken charge of the last time they worked.

"You know if there were a way, I'd get our old Sarge back," Jared responded.

"Yeah, I know," Alex said. "I'm kidding. I mean, damn. Kidding but not really kidding. He's on the Kool-aid bad, huh? I didn't want to believe all the rumors were true, but I saw it firsthand, and now I'm nervous to be at work with him."

"Maybe he'll lighten up," Jared said. "Maybe he's just trying to puff out his chest or something. I don't know. But we'll find a way to work with him. We have a good shift, we can handle a crappy supervisor. You know?"

Alex nodded. "Yeah. Yeah, I know."

"Time to get in there, Mang, and start our day," Jared said. They walked in to work, both bracing themselves for how their new Sergeant would act next.

"Bravo 400s, welcome to another lovely day at work," Trey said at the start of show-up. "I already really like you guys." He looked around, looked at Mandy, and added, "And gal." He flashed a fake-looking smile with his obviously bleached teeth.

"Today's BOLO is up on the projector, you can all read, right? Just check it out before you leave. And that's all I have. I'll be out and about, backing some of you up as the evening goes along, because I enjoy being an involved supervisor. Some of you know this already." He stopped and looked at Robbie. Smiled at him. Looked over at Alex, who was sitting a few rows over. Smiled at him too.

Awkward, Alex mouthed to Robbie after Sarge looked away.

"So. Have a great night, everyone. Get to work."

Walking out to patrol cars, Corey caught up to Brandon to stop him. "Hey, dude, ready for camping?"

"You know I am," Brandon answered him. "I'm looking forward to it. Only two weekends away now. Can't wait."

"It's good timing, right? I mean, we have this squirrely new Sarge, and that's been crappy, and we'll get to go before you have a new kid and can't get out anymore . . ."

Brandon laughed. "Yeah, I won't get out for a little while, not while he's a newborn anyway. Gotta help the wife."

"How much time you taking off of work?"

"Oh, three or four weeks, man," Brandon answered. "I have plenty of time to use."

"Yeah, three or four will be good. That's about what I've done. Took off a month each time to be there with Cassie."

"Well. I guess it's that time," Brandon said. "Want to have seven together later? Maybe some greasy dinner from Floyd's?"

"Sounds good, man," Corey answered. "I could go for some chicken fried steak smothered in gravy. I'll text you when I'm going, see if you can go at the same time."

"Deal."

They entered their separate patrol cars then, and started their evenings.

They hadn't been on the road for more than five minutes when a domestic dispute call came out. Corey checked the address on the computer in his patrol car—he recalled the house number right away. He had been there before, with Robbie. They'd seen a woman who was clearly beaten up by someone, presumably her boyfriend, but she refused to get help or press charges. Missy, her name was. Yes, Corey remembered that her name was Missy. He also remembered the blood on her shirt. He recalled how upset she became with her neighbor for calling them out there.

"This again," Corey said, thinking out loud. "Okay. What has happened to Missy today?"

He took the call alone, believing it would be the same situation as before with this couple. He showed up to the house—but this time, there *was* a car in the driveway. So the boyfriend hadn't bailed yet. Perhaps this time he could hook this guy up, take him to jail. Perhaps this would be the day she pressed charges.

No one was outside this time, either. He looked over at the neighbor's house, the one who had been outside last time. She wasn't there. He knocked on the front door three times. "Officer Corey Hayes, CCPD," he said loudly.

Nothing. He knocked again. Announced his arrival again. "Officer Corey Hayes, CCPD, open up."

He listened intently at the door. He heard nothing except the wind outside at first. Then he heard a muffled scream. He knew he had to take action. He quickly called for backup. "Forcing entry now," he said on the radio. He unholstered his gun as he kicked in the locked door. As soon as the door was forced in with Corey's boot, he saw Missy on the floor. Her boyfriend held a gun to her head with his right hand and his left covered her mouth. Corey aimed his Glock 17 but was hesitant because he didn't want to hit Missy. The boyfriend pulled his trigger first. A single gunshot fired out, hitting Corey in his neck. He immediately fell to the ground.

Missy looked over at Corey in horror and screamed. Her voice was silenced by another round as it went through her brain.

The man got up, walked over to an unconscious Corey, and shot him a second time, in the head. "Pig," he said, stepping over his body and heading to another room in the house.

Lights and sirens lit up outside the house as Corey's backup arrived. He had called for them on the radio only two minutes prior. Brandon was the first on scene. He ran up the steps and into the house. He saw Corey's boots on the ground before he saw anything else from the open door. He knew right away that Corey was down. He just knew. "Officer down," he frantically called on the radio as he unholstered his gun. He made entry into the house, gun drawn. He saw the pool of blood surrounding Corey. He saw Missy too, and her brains splattered to the left of her, on the living room wall.

"Where are you, bastard?" Brandon whispered as he began searching for the man who did this. The man who took his brother. The man who killed his best friend. It didn't take long for him to find him. The boyfriend had gone into the master bedroom, sat on his bed, and shot himself in the head. "Son of a bitch," Brandon said. "You took that away from me." He got on his radio again. "Suspect is down. Self-inflicted gunshot wound to the head."

He ran back into the living room to where Corey was. Stood over his body. "No, no, no," he said. "No, brother. You can't leave me. We're supposed to go camping, man. We have plans."

He knew, though, that Corey's soul had already departed. He was too late. "We should have ridden out together today, brother," he said. "I'm so sorry I wasn't here for you . . . I'm so sorry." Tears welled in his eyes. "I'm sorry, man. I'm so sorry."

More lights and sirens. Mandy Jacobs ran up. She looked at Corey and put her hand over her heart as if to save it from coming out of her chest. "Oh, no, no," she said. "Hayes! Hayes! NO!" She put her arm around Brandon. "Morgan, I can't believe this. I can't believe he's gone. This can't be happening . . ." Her tears started to fall then too. "Our brother. Our brother's gone."

Brandon knew he needed to pull it together. Every cop had other cops assigned to be the ones to go to their homes in the event of losing their lives in the line of duty, to inform the family. He had assigned Corey and Corey had assigned him. It was just always a hypothetical. He never imagined he would have to face Cassie with this news.

Later he stood on Cassie's doorstep. The command chaplain and Sergeant Johnson accompanied him. One doorbell ring and he stood and waited. One of the kids had recently colored with sidewalk chalk on their porch. He stood there, staring at the picture of a sun and stick figures. A pair of Mackenzie's neon pink sandals was on the porch, as well. *Please, let those kids be in bed,* Brandon thought to himself.

Jacob answered the door. The boy's eyebrows went down with a visibly confused look. "Hey, what are you doing here, Mr. Brandon?" he said. Cassie came up then, right behind him.

"Brandon, hey," she said. She looked at the command chaplain, saw the silver cross pin on his uniform. Saw the new Sarge. Looked again at Brandon's face. Suddenly, she knew. They didn't have to say anything.

She started breathing hard and shaking her head. "No."

"Mom, what's wrong?" Jacob asked.

"No, no . . ." She couldn't say anything else. She started to take steps backward, away from them. She continued to shake her head.

Brandon went to Jacob to lead him away as the Chaplain and Sergeant Johnson walked over to Cassie. They led her to another place where she could sit and found the kitchen table. They helped her into a chair.

"Hey, Jacob, where are your sister and brother?" Brandon asked.

"Watching TV in the living room," he said. "It's Friday. Mom lets us stay up late watching movies on Fridays."

"I want for you to go with them for a minute while I talk to your mom," he said.

"Okay," Jacob said. He didn't understand, but obeyed and walked into the living room.

Brandon walked back over. It was obvious that the Chaplain and Sarge had just officially told her of Corey's passing. Cassie's body went limp and fell out of the kitchen chair, onto her knees. "No, Brandon," she said. "No. This can't be. No." She began to sob. "Oh, God, why? Why?" She sobbed more.

Brandon leaned down to her level, put his hand over her back. "I'm so sorry, Cassie," he said. He clenched his teeth, shifted his jaw. Took a deep breath. He couldn't break down. This was his job, to be there and be strong for her. Corey had assigned him to do this, and he would. "We are all going to be here for you, to help you. Okay? You won't be alone. We're here."

She started heaving then. She ran to the guest bathroom and lost her dinner.

***

"EVERYONE NEEDS TO GET out of here," Corporal Harris said to the Bravo 400s at the end of that shift. "I know it's hard to go home after a night like this. But you need to get home. Get to your families."

Nothing else was said. It was completely silent as everyone walked out to the parking lot; the only sounds heard were car keys being pulled out from pockets and boots shuffling on the cement ground. Chris took his backpack off to throw it in his trunk, hit the unlock button on his keys, and then froze as he looked up at his car. He had parked right next to Corey's truck that day. He broke down then, keys in one hand, backpack in the other. He was unable to move. His eyes were locked on to the truck Corey wouldn't be getting into that night, or ever again.

It hadn't quite registered for him yet, that Corey was gone. He hadn't allowed his mind to process it. But looking at his truck then, knowing Corey should be getting in it and driving home to his family too—that did it. He stood there, unable to move forward and walk to his car. He stood behind Corey's truck and was stuck.

"I just gave Hayes crap for driving a Ford last week," Joe said, walking up to Chris, his eyes on Corey's truck. He opened his mouth again to speak, but lost his words suddenly, and was just silent instead. He saw that Chris was crying. He patted his back. "You need to get home, brother. Get home to Kristin and the kids."

Chris looked at Joe in the eyes then. "Yeah," he said in a voice just above a whisper. "Yeah, Zavala, you're right."

Joe just nodded at him and patted him on the back one more time. Then he walked over to Corey's truck and touched the side, leaving his hand there a moment and bowing his head. Then he walked across the parking lot to his own car. It was time to go home for the day.

***

FIVE DAYS PASSED AND THE SUN didn't shine on any of them, not a single one. The morning of the funeral it was raining. It was a light rain, but a steady one, the type of rainy day Cassie would normally long for. She imagined if Corey were here now, they would make a lazy day out of it, watching Netflix all day, making popcorn. Relaxing. But he wasn't here. And he'd never be here again with her, with their children. How could that be? Leah was there at the Hayes house that morning. She'd been by Cassie's side non-stop, not an easy task for a woman who was already busy with two little girls and due soon with a new baby. Leah's parents had taken the girls so she could be there for her friend. It all seemed surreal, Corey being gone. Cassie felt like she was living out a scene of a movie—not real life—as she stared out her bedroom window at the drizzling rain.

"Cass, it's time to get dressed," Leah softly said, holding up the black A-line dress Cassie would be wearing to her husband's funeral.

Cassie turned her attention from the window and looked at the dress. "I actually wore this to a wedding last fall," Cassie said, taking the dress from Leah. She stepped into it, stood at the mirror a bit, and caressed her hand over the fabric. "It was my cousin's wedding, in San Antonio. My mom took the kids for the night. We had so much fun at that wedding, and then at the Riverwalk after . . . if I'd have known then that the next time I'd wear this dress, it would be for . . . for Corey's funeral . . ."

She stopped. Leah put her hand over Cassie's back. Cassie's mother, Janice, walked in then. "Cassandra, the kids are dressed and ready to go," she said. "Is there anything I can do to help you get ready?"

"Leah's helping, just be with the kids, Mama," Cassie said. Outside, thunder rolled. "Actually—the umbrellas are in the garage. You could grab those, please."

Janice walked over and kissed Cassie's forehead. "Will do, Cassandra." She smiled at Leah and walked out the door.

"Corey said we have too many umbrellas," Cassie said, sitting on the edge of her bed then. "He made fun of me for having too many. We got in a fight over it one time. Actually, pretty recently. He cleaned out the garage last month. Yes, it was last month. Spring cleaning. He tried to donate a couple of umbrellas to Goodwill and I told him no. I don't know why I told him no. Stupid fight. Stupid, stupid fight." She looked down at her left ring finger then. Twisted the ring around a few times. Leah could tell she was trembling.

"We should be getting ready for the guys' camping trip, Leah. That's what we *should* be doing. Not this. I don't want this to be real. It's not fair. I want Corey to come home. I keep closing my eyes really hard . . . like if I close them hard enough, when I open them, this will have all been a terrible nightmare and he'll be home. But I open my eyes and this is my reality and I can't stand it. It's not fair. Nothing about this is fair, Leah. None of it."

She started sobbing then. Her face was red and veins were visibly puffy under her eyes. She struggled to catch her breath. She put her head in her hands. "I miss him already," she said through tears. "I don't know how to do this. I don't know how I'll get through this."

Leah rubbed Cassie's back gently. What could she possibly say? She was struggling to keep from choking up herself.

"I'm here," is all she could manage to get out, quietly, calmly, as if she were consoling one of her children. "I'm here."

A gentle knock on the bedroom door caused Cassie to sit up then. "Come in," she managed to say.

In walked Phil, Corey's father, retired Dallas PD officer. He was wearing his dress uniform. Seeing the name HAYES sketched on his nameplate caused Leah to quickly look away, as she didn't want to start crying. Not now, not in front of Cassie.

"Irene and I will be in the car right behind you," he said to his daughter-in-law, putting a hand on her shoulder.

She looked up at him and nodded.

Phil sighed. "I came in here with the intent to say more than that." He sat down next to her then, putting his elbows on his knees and his face in his hands.

"This is hard," he said. "Really hard. You, Cassie—you're too young to be a widow. My grandchildren are too young to lose their father. And Irene and I, we never thought we'd have to bury a child."

Cassie just sat there, staring off into nothing. Phil sat up straight then, and put his arm around her shoulder.

"But I'm damn proud of my son. I'm damn proud of you too, Cassie."

He stood up and began to exit the room. "We'll all get through this, together," he said.

Janice appeared at Cassie's bedroom door then. "Cassandra, it's almost time," she said. "The car is waiting outside for us."

She looked at her mom through her tears and nodded. She stood up. "Okay," she said. "I'm as ready as I'm going to be." Janice linked her arm in Cassie's and helped her walk out. Cassie turned back to Leah. "Thank you so much, Leah. For everything. I'll see you there, I guess."

Leah nodded. "Of course," she said.

Leah watched Cassie, Janice, and the kids being helped into a black Tahoe that would transport them to the church. She watched Phil open the door of his truck for Irene, who wore a black veil over her face. After watching both vehicles drive away she finally helped herself into her own car, and headed to the church.

CHAPTER 22

THE CHIEF HAD JUST FINISHED his speech. Leah thought that was it, that this part of the funeral would be over now. She was surprised to see her husband, as well as the rest of the Bravo 400s, stand up and make their way to the podium. Brandon hadn't told her that this was going to happen. Brandon stood in front. Leah was zoned in on his face, trying to read it. He began to speak.

"I had the privilege not only to work with Officer Hayes, but to know him outside of work too, and to know his family." Brandon started to choke up and had to take a moment to continue.

"Words fail me now. There is no easy way to say goodbye to this man—my friend—a fine officer, a fine husband, a fine father. I just know he will always be a member of this police department . . . proudly serving us, this time in Heaven as one of God's sheepdogs. Rest easy, my brother. We have the watch."

Both Brandon and Leah allowed their tears to fall then as Brandon and the rest of the shift slowly walked off the stage. It now was time to go to the burial plot. Leah watched as officers all around her stood and began to exit the church. She put her hand over her belly. Her son was moving around like crazy in there, which was a welcome distraction. She took a deep breath and looked down at her black ballerina flats. She tried to mentally prepare herself to get up on her feet and begin the walk back to her car, which would be followed by a drive to the cemetery.

"You okay?" the woman sitting next to her said. She had been looking at Leah's burgeoning belly as she asked.

"Fine," Leah responded. "As fine as can be, I guess."

The woman put her hand down to help Leah to her feet. She accepted the help. Leah looked over at the front of the church and saw Cassie and the kids being escorted out by Brandon and the other shift-mates. She saw Cassie's face, briefly. She looked okay. She did. *We'll help her through this,* Leah thought. *We'll be here.* She hoped that Cassie could feel that. The support all around her.

And she did. Through her grief, Cassie felt the love and support surrounding her. Her heart was broken, but she knew she wasn't alone. She stared out the window during the funeral procession for her husband as they traveled from the church to the cemetery. The rain that had been steadily falling since morning ceased and the sun was starting to peek out from behind gray clouds. Cassie had seen footage of cops' funeral processions on the news before, but nothing like this. People were just standing outside, lining the roads. Many saluted the hearse as it drove by. She felt a moment of pride then, despite her sadness. *They are saluting my husband,* she thought to herself. She looked at her kids, and then directed their attention to the crowds of people lining the street. "Kids, look out the window," she said, pointing. "Those people out there, they are standing up, saluting your daddy."

All three kids looked out. Jacob had a single tear fall down his cheek. "I want Dad," he said. Mackenzie looked out at the people lining the road, and then at her mother. "Daddy is a hero, that is what everyone is saying," she said.

Cassie nodded. "Yes, that is right," she said. "He is a hero. And I know, Jacob. I want him too."

She got a tissue out of her bag and handed it to her son. She got one out for herself too. Her kids' sadness was heavy. She couldn't hold back her own tears, watching theirs. She wiped her face and blew her nose.

Janice spoke then. "You know, Cassandra, Corey went to the place that all of us will be going to. He just walked before us is all. But we'll all be with him again, when God says it's time."

Cassie smiled at her mom. "Yeah, Mama, you're right. You're totally right." She looked at her kids again. "We will be okay, kids, I promise," she said through the tears. "We'll be okay."

The cars came to a stop. She was helped out of her car by Corporal Harris. The entire shift was standing there, waiting. They all watched Cassie and the kids exit the car.

Cassie was led to her seat in front of the burial plot. She walked in front of the honor guard as they began to play the bagpipes. Her husband's coffin was slowly taken out of the hearse by his shift-mates. She inhaled, slowly, as his coffin was brought over and then was set down. She watched intently as an officer in the honor guard methodically removed the flag from the casket, folding it perfectly, and then holding it across his chest. The Chief marched over to him, saluted the flag, and then carefully accepted it as it was transferred to his arms. The Chief did an about-face turn, and slowly walked over to Cassie and her children, that flag tightly held across his chest. He knelt down in front of her and placed the flag in Cassie's lap. She held on tight to that flag, her body still trembling. She longed to be holding onto her husband, not to a flag.

Officers around all stood at attention as the radio traffic began. It was time for Corey's final 42, his last call. A dispatcher called out, "Corpus Christi Police Department 404?"

Silence. Deafening silence.

Again. "Corpus Christi Police Department 404?"

She'd never longed to hear his voice answer that call like she did then, hearing dispatch call out a third time, "Corpus Christi Police Department 404?" She closed her eyes and put her head down.

How many seconds passed after the third call? Cassie couldn't be sure. She took a deep breath, opened her eyes, and looked at the faces of her children.

Dispatch started up again. "Last call—Corpus Christi Police Department 404, status 42. End of watch, date May 5, 2017, 1500 hours." A quick break. The dispatcher's voice was breaking up. "'There is no greater love than a man who would lay down his life for another. John 15:13.' Corpus Christi Officer Corey Hayes, Badge number 4278, is ten-forty-two. He has gone home for the final time. Godspeed, my brother."

EPILOGUE

6 MONTHS AFTER THE FUNERAL

"CONGRATULATIONS, PERALES," Brian said to Danny, shaking his hand, at Danny's wedding reception.

"Thanks, White," he said. "Appreciate it. Hey, White—Sierra's bridesmaids are seriously all single. You should go talk to one of them."

"Oh, heck, maybe I will," Brian replied. "But I need some liquid courage first. Open bar—right? Hey, let me bring you and your wife a drink."

Sierra smiled at him. "Thanks, Brian," she said. "I'll have a glass of wine. My husband, he'll have a beer." She giggled. "Wow. Feels cool to say husband."

Danny pulled her in for a kiss. "Feels cool to say wife, *my darling wife*," he said with a grin.

Leah walked into the reception area from the bathroom with her five-month-old son in her arms. "Now that you have a fresh diaper, let's go congratulate the new couple, buddy," she said, walking over to Danny and Sierra. Brandon joined them.

Brandon shook Danny's hand, and Leah hugged Sierra. "Welcome to the married club, brother," Brandon said. "Congratulations."

"Thanks, brother," Danny said. "I mean, I should be congratulating you too though, man. *Detective* Morgan. Congrats on the promotion."

"Hey, thanks," Brandon replied. "I'm excited. I'll miss you guys on the shift though."

"We'll miss you too, but I'm happy for you, man."

"Well, thanks again," Brandon said. "But today is about you two."

"Yes, it's about you two," Leah said. "Congratulations." She held out the baby. "Little Corey says congrats too." She smiled as Sierra snatched him up.

"Baby Corey has really grown since the last time I saw him," Sierra said. "I swear he gets cuter and cuter, if that's possible. And . . . wait . . . do I see a tooth?"

Leah nodded and smiled. "Yes, my baby has his first tooth already," she said. "It's going too fast."

"Awww," Sierra said. She handed baby Corey back over after kissing his cheek. "Well, thanks for being here, guys. It means a lot."

"We wouldn't miss it," Leah said. "You two are family."

Cassie walked into the reception hall with Jacob, Mackenzie, and Noah. She was greeted warmly by everyone. Danny and Sierra noticed her and walked over right away.

Cassie smiled as they approached her. "Sierra, wow, you are such a beautiful bride," she said. Sierra hugged her. "And I have to tell you, I love that you chose to have a December wedding. The poinsettias are gorgeous."

Danny hugged her next. "Congratulations, Danny," Cassie said. "I'm so happy for you."

"Thank you so much, Cassie," Danny told her. "We're really glad you're here. We're glad the kids are here too. We wanted to do something special for Corey today." He took her arm in his and began walking. "We left a spot for him at your table."

They led her over to a round table with eight chairs. She saw Corey's spot right away. One of his uniform blouses was draped over the back of the chair. There was a candle burning, a single blue flower in a vase, an empty place setting, and a bottle of beer. His badge number—4278—was sketched onto a card propped up in front of the place setting.

Cassie smiled at them both. "Thank you for this," she said, then turned her head back to look at his empty chair. She held her fingers to her mouth. She shook her head. Her eyes became glossy with tears. Shift-mates began walking over and taking turns hugging Cassie.

"We're so glad you're here," she heard over and over again.

"I wouldn't miss this," Cassie replied. "You're all family."

Even Sergeant Gabe Torres had come to the wedding, though he hadn't been Danny Perales's supervisor since April. Cassie was happy to see him as he and Eva walked up.

"Sarge, it's so great to see you," she said as he came in for a hug.

"Great to see you, as well, Cassie," he said. "Is everyone here taking good care of you?"

"Oh, that's an understatement," she said. "It's been overwhelming, the support from everyone. Just last week Jacob had a Boy Scout camping trip, and both Brandon Morgan and Chris Janacek accompanied him, because normally Corey would, and Jacob almost didn't want to go this year. They talked to him and convinced him. He ended up having a really good time. There is a father-daughter dance every February—I know that's still a couple of months away—but Brandon Morgan has already agreed to take Mack for me. He was always kind of a second dad anyway, he and Corey were so close." She looked over at Brandon and Leah then. "I guess you heard they named their son after Corey?" she asked him.

"Oh, wow, I did not know that," Gabe answered. "But that's really wonderful. Really wonderful, indeed. I do remember how close Officer Morgan and Officer Hayes were. I'm glad to hear your families are remaining that close."

Cassie nodded. "I don't have to tell you, Sarge, this blue family is a forever family."

He nodded and smiled. "That it is," he replied. "It sure is."

CPSIA information can be obtained
at www.ICGtesting.com
Printed in the USA
BVHW03s1834070318
509964BV00001B/105/P

9 781632 134769